'Come in,' Matro

Daisy took in a ragge   mouthed softly.

He inclined his head slightly. 'Daisy...this *is* a surprise.'

Matron, seeming not to notice his coolness, said in a pleased voice, 'How splendid—you two know each other already.'

'Yes,' Daisy murmured, 'we're old——'

'Acquaintances,' broke in the doctor, letting her know by uttering that single word that he didn't wish to acknowledge the close friendship that had once existed between them.

Kids. . .one of life's joys, one of life's treasures.

Kisses. . .of warmth, kisses of passion, kisses from mothers and kisses from lovers.

In *Kids & Kisses*. . .every story has it all.

Margaret O'Neill started scribbling at four and began nursing at twenty. She contracted TB and, when recovered, did her British Tuberculosis Association nursing training before general training at the Royal Portsmouth Hospital. She married, had two children, and with her late husband she owned and managed several nursing homes. Now retired and living in Sussex, she still has many nursing contacts. Her husband would have been delighted to see her books in print.

Recent titles by the same author:

NO LONGER A STRANGER
TAKE A DEEP BREATH
LONG HOT SUMMER
NEVER PAST LOVING
CHRISTMAS IS FOREVER

DOWNLAND CLINIC

BY
MARGARET O'NEILL

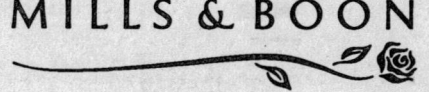

DID YOU PURCHASE THIS BOOK WITHOUT A COVER?

If you did, you should be aware it is **stolen property** as it was reported *unsold and destroyed* by a retailer. Neither the Author nor the publisher has received any payment for this book.

All the characters in this book have no existence outside the imagination of the author, and have no relation whatsoever to anyone bearing the same name or names. They are not even distantly inspired by any individual known or unknown to the author, and all the incidents are pure invention.

All rights reserved. The text of this publication or any part thereof may not be reproduced or transmitted in any form or by any means, electronic or mechanical, including photocopying, recording, storage in an information retrieval system, or otherwise, without the written permission of the publisher.

This book is sold subject to the condition that it shall not, by way of trade or otherwise, be lent, resold, hired out or otherwise circulated without the prior consent of the publisher in any form of binding or cover other than that in which it is published and without a similar condition including this condition being imposed on the subsequent purchaser.

MILLS & BOON, the Rose Device and LOVE ON CALL are trademarks of the publisher.
Harlequin Mills & Boon Limited,
Eton House, 18–24 Paradise Road, Richmond, Surrey TW9 1SR
This edition published by arrangement with
Harlequin Enterprises B.V.

© Margaret O'Neill 1995

ISBN 0 263 79361 3

Set in 10 on 12 pt Linotron Times
03-9510-55451

Typeset in Great Britain by CentraCet, Cambridge
Made and printed in Great Britain

CHAPTER ONE

A STRONG wind buffeted Daisy's car as she drove slowly eastwards along the cliff road, leaving the town of Brighthelm behind her. She drove slowly, partly on account of the wind blowing in off the choppy sea, and partly because she didn't want to be too early for her interview at Featherston Hall Clinic, commonly known, because of its geographical position, as 'Downland Clinic'.

Her second interview, she reminded herself as a little frisson of excitement coursed through her. Today was to be decision time. She was one of three short-listed from the large group of applicants who had been interviewed a month ago.

She allowed her thoughts to stray back over the last few weeks and her introduction to Featherston Hall.

Although she had known herself to be well-qualified to fill the post as relief sister and assistant matron at the clinic, she had applied for the job with some misgivings because of her personal history. Would the matron, Mrs Browning, owner of the large clinic which catered for private and referred National Health patients, even consider employing a thirty-three-year-old widow with an eight-year-old son, when there were plenty of single, unencumbered women around, equally well-qualified?

She hadn't been able even to begin to guess at what the matron's response might be, but had felt impelled to answer the advertisement, as it was a perfect solution to her problem of being a single working mother. An interesting, well-paid, responsible job, with a two-bedroomed staff bungalow on offer, if needed. 'Married couple with dependant welcome to apply,' the advertisement had read. Was it possible that the welcome would be extended to a single parent? Daisy had wondered.

Well, she had been short-listed, which meant that Matron and the elderly, soon-to-retire medical officer hadn't turned her down out of hand at her first interview. That was something in her favour. In fact, she had sensed that Mrs Browning was sympathetic to her situation, once she had established that she was otherwise suitable for the post. She had even been complimentary about the efforts Daisy was making to do her utmost for Rupert.

'It is difficult enough,' the matron had said at her first interview, 'for a couple to bring up children, but doubly difficult for a single parent to cope. You must have found it particularly hard work when you were first widowed. How old was Rupert when his father died?'

'Nearly a year. But I was lucky, I had a marvellous aunt who offered us a home, and offered to help look after Rupert so that I could return to nursing. It enabled me to do midwifery, and do a clinical management course, and get in plenty of practical nursing experience in the general field for which I was trained.'

For a brief moment, Daisy had considered explaining that she had in fact left her late husband, Matthew, before he died, because she'd been afraid for herself and her son; but the matter was too complicated, too hurtful and private to explain. The moment had passed; it really had nothing to do with her application for this job. Let the sympathetic matron believe that she had moved in with her aunt because she had been widowed. Surely this small deception couldn't hurt anybody, and now that dear Aunt Mary was no longer alive nobody but herself would ever know anything about her unhappy marriage. And one other, a small voice in the back of her head had whispered—Matthew's one-time best friend, who blamed her for the break-up of their marriage and for breaking his friend's heart, and from whom she had parted so bitterly.

Quickly she had squashed the memory.

'And what's happened to change what seems like an ideal arrangement?' Dr Harris, the elderly medical officer, had asked, breaking in on her unpleasant thoughts.

Somehow, Daisy had pulled herself together. Overwhelmed with grief for a moment, for past and present sadness, she had had to swallow hard, before answering. 'My aunt was killed in a road accident a few weeks ago,' she had explained, 'and her son, who inherited the house, wants to sell, so I have to find other accommodation. In any case, I need to work somewhere where Rupert can be catered for when I am on duty, and I understand from the information you sent me that you have crêche and child-care facilities here.'

'Yes, we pride ourselves on taking care of our staff,' matron had said, with a warm smile. 'And I'm sure that should you be working when the facilities are closed you would always find a resident off-duty member of staff willing to keep an eye on your son.'

'That's what I was hoping,' Daisy had replied, returning Mrs Browning's smile.

Daisy remembered that smile now, how kind and reassuring it had been. She realised that Matron reminded her of her aunt, though not in looks. Her aunt had been much older, with her grey hair worn short, whereas Helen Browning was only in her early fifties, and wore her shining, chestnut-coloured hair in a sophisticated chignon. But there was something about her manner that was as warm and embracing as Aunt Mary's.

A great surge of optimism washed over her. She knew that she had already formed a rapport with Mrs Browning and suddenly she felt confident that she had a good chance of getting this job. Featherston Hall was so perfect for herself and Rupert, she just had to be successful.

Tummy churning, heart thumping madly, she realised that she had reached the lane that led up to where the clinic stood, tucked into a fold in the downs, a grand, thirties-style mansion, much enlarged, looking out over the stormy sea. She had dawdled long enough; time to face her interview with the sympathetic matron and the slightly crusty old medical officer.

In fact, a short while later when she was shown into Matron's office, it was to find that lady alone.

'Poor Dr Harris had a slight heart attack a couple of weeks ago,' Mrs Browning explained as she shook hands with Daisy, 'and has already retired, but his assistant, Dr Delaney, who is also our anaesthetist, has been competently holding the fort. Our replacement medical officer is due some time today, but has not yet arrived, so I decided to hold these second interviews on my own. In any case, the new medical officer could hardly contribute much on his own first day, could he?' she finished with a smile.

'Hardly,' replied Daisy, returning the smile, and privately rejoicing that there was to be no third party present; she found Matron so easy to talk to. 'I'm so sorry to hear about Dr Harris. Is he making a good recovery?'

'Splendid, I'm happy to say. We had him in our medical unit for a few days, but he was discharged home last week, and is looking forward to a holiday, which he badly needs. Life here at Featherston has been pretty hectic recently, what with enlarging the surgical wing and losing my assistant matron, on whom I relied heavily. But when her husband was suddenly posted abroad, she naturally had to go with him. I don't blame her—families come first—but I miss her. Grace was a wizard at juggling staff when we were short-handed, and always willing to fill in herself at short notice, as I am sure you would be, Mrs Marchment.'

Daisy inclined her head. 'Naturally,' she said. 'In fact I'm looking forward to some hands-on nursing as well as administrative work.'

'Good, now tell me, if you found yourself short of, say, two members of nursing staff, a sister and an auxiliary, would you. . .?'

So they slipped easily into interviewing mode, with Daisy hardly noticing. Mostly she found herself agreeing with the matron over what one should do in certain situations, but occasionally she disagreed, however reluctantly. Yet she had to say what was in her mind, and hope that she didn't spoil her chances by so doing. Apparently she didn't, because at the end of half an hour Mrs Browning said, 'I think we've talked enough, Mrs Marchment—Daisy—do you mind if I call you Daisy?'

Daisy shook her head, and her bobbed bell of pale daffodil-yellow hair gleamed in the lamplight, a bright spot in the gloom of the winter afternoon. 'Of course not,' she replied. 'I should like that.' Her pulses quickened. Did that mean. . .?

'Good,' replied Matron, smiling as her cool grey eyes met Daisy's. 'Because I think we are going to be seeing a lot of each other in the future. You're my last interviewee, and I'm offering you the post of assistant matron and relief sister at Featherston Hall. That is if you still want the job after the grilling I've just given you?' Her smile broadened.

Daisy's heart somersaulted. She beamed at Mrs Browning, her violet-blue eyes shining with happiness. 'Oh, Matron, of course I want it. I just know that I'm going to love working here, and with you.'

'Yes, I believe we have already formed some sort of rapport, which is important, for I shall rely on you heavily, Daisy, just as I do on Liz, my secretary. She has been with me for many years and is an absolute tower of strength, as was old Dr Harris when my husband died and I decided to carry on alone. I just hope that my new medical officer is as supportive. He is well-qualified, and seems an extremely pleasant young man; we took to each other on sight, much as you and I did.'

'Young?'

'Well, not so young—in his late thirties. He's very ambitious, which is why he's interested in the clinic; he knows that I want to expand over the next few years, and he wants to be in on the planning stage. He is a consultant physician, and will be doing some consultative work for the local hospitals in Brighthelm, but he will be resident here, in the lodge, and will be working principally for the clinic. I expect you and and he to work closely together. I have such a lot of admin work to do that I will be off-loading much of the executive practical work on to you, like the daily round for instance.'

'I look forward to doing that, the sooner——' The internal telephone rang.

With a murmured, 'Excuse me,' Matron picked up the receiver. 'Well, how fortuitous,' she said, raising her eyebrows at Daisy. 'Send him in straight away; it couldn't be better timing.' She put down the receiver. 'Would you believe,' she said, smiling, 'that our new medical officer has just arrived? So you will meet him today after all.'

'Oh, great,' said Daisy, looking towards the door as somebody tapped at it.

'Come in,' Matron called, and the door opened.

A tall, lean-figured man in a grey suit stood for a moment framed in the doorway. He was smiling pleasantly, confidently, displaying gleaming, even teeth in a handsome, tanned face. Thick black wiry hair sprang vibrantly from a high forehead.

Daisy stared at him, and took in a ragged breath. 'Adam!' she mouthed softly. 'Adam Torrence.'

CHAPTER TWO

DAISY'S *sotto voce* exclamation seemed to have passed unnoticed.

'Do come in, Dr Torrence,' said Matron pleasantly, holding out her hand. 'Welcome to Featherston Hall. You couldn't have arrived at a better time; there's someone here I want you to meet.'

For a moment the new arrival paused in the doorway, taking in the scene before him, his dark eyes resting first on Matron seated behind her desk, and then on Daisy. Momentarily a look of recognition and astonishment flickered across his face as he glanced at Daisy, and then it was gone. His smile didn't falter as he crossed the room and shook Matron's hand in greeing.

'Good afternoon,' he said in the rich, warm, baritone voice that Daisy remembered so well. 'It's good to be here. I'm looking forward to taking up the reins of office. Sorry I couldn't take over immediately Dr Harris fell ill, but as you know I was committed elsewhere until now.' He turned and looked down at Daisy, who was sitting staring at this ghost from her past in stunned amazement. He inclined his head slightly. 'Daisy, Mrs Marchment—it is still Mrs Marchment, isn't it?' he asked with cool formality. Daisy nodded mutely. 'This *is* a surprise.' He held out a hand and, as if mesmerised, she slipped hers into it, meeting his gaze as she did so. His eyes were dark, fathomless, unreadable pools.

Matron, seeming not to notice his coolness, said in a

pleased voice, 'How splendid; so there's no need for introductions—you two know each other already.'

Daisy felt the blood rush to her cheeks and then drain from them. She felt quite faint for a moment. Her heart thumped unevenly. She found her voice and forced a smile to her lips. 'Yes,' she murmured, 'we're old——'

'Acquaintances,' broke in the doctor, letting her know by uttering that single word that he didn't wish to acknowledge the close friendship that had once existed between them. 'Daisy and her late husband and I were together at the same training hospital.'

Matron beamed. 'Of course, you were both at St Vincent's; it was mentioned in your cvs. How wonderful that you know each other and have worked together before. I must say it augurs well for the future that our new medical officer and new assistant matron are already acquainted, and there's always some sort of a bond when you've trained at the same hospital. Nothing could be better.'

Adam said pleasantly but drily, 'But you shouldn't read too much into that, Matron. We were very junior in those days, you know, hot-blooded youth and all that, and a lot of water has passed under the bridge since then.'

'Nevertheless, you know something about each other on a personal level. That's important. It should make for a splendid working relationship.'

'Unless,' said Adam, one eyebrow arched in a quizzical manner, 'we have both changed out of all recognition. That's possible, you know, Mrs Browning.' He spoke half teasingly but, to Daisy's ears, half seriously, warningly. Or was she imagining it?

'If you have, my instinct tells me it has been for the better,' said Matron with a laugh. She turned to Daisy.

'What do you think, my dear? Have you changed much in the intervening years?'

After a moment, Daisy, still extraordinarily shocked by this unexpected and unwelcome meeting with Adam, cleared her throat, and said rather stiltedly, 'Yes, I believe that I have, and hopefully for the better. Losing my husband when I was young and bringing up a child virtually single-handed have helped me do that.' She turned and looked at Adam, her direct gaze willing him to understand that Matron believed her to be a bereft young widow and not a woman, however provoked, who had left her husband voluntarily. She hoped that he would get the message and, producing a smile of sorts, asked softly, meaningfully, 'And you, Adam, do you feel that work and experience have matured you and given you a better, perhaps more sympathetic understanding of people and their problems?'

'Naturally,' he said. 'I am more cautious in my judgements than I was when younger—although some youthful judgements are not necessarily wrong, are they?' His voice was neutral, but he looked at her with hard eyes.

Was this another warning, letting her know that he still felt bitterly angry about the way she had walked out on Matthew? It sounded like it. She squashed the frightening thought, and replied, with a little laugh for Matron's benefit, 'No, that's true, they're not. But the young to do tend to make rash judgements, don't they? Due perhaps to misplaced loyalty. They so often think only with their hearts and not with their heads, don't you think?'

Adam's lip curled up at the corner. 'There's nothing wrong with a bit of heart in the right place, although you make it sound as if we only grow heartless as we get older,' he said silkily, 'but that's surely not the prerogative of age, is it? The young can be heartless too. What do you think, Mrs Browning?' he asked, turning a bland face to Matron.

Matron laughed and looked from one to the other of them. 'I think that you two are old friends and old sparring partners,' she said with a smile, unaware of the true bitterness of the barbs they were aiming at each other. 'But you'll have to thrash out this particular argument on another occasion. I don't know what you would like to do, Dr Torrence; perhaps you want to get settled in the lodge? But if not, I'm taking Daisy off to look round the clinic again and meet a few people, and you're welcome to join us if you wish. Of course, I realise that you'll want to see Dr Delaney as soon as possible, and discuss cases, but he's in Theatre at the moment, anaesthetising for Mr Black, our gynae consultant. They're doing a laparotomy on a query ovarian cancer patient, and a couple of other ops this afternoon, so he won't be free for a bit.'

'Then I'll do a tour of inspection with you if I may, and introduce myself to patients, and staff whom I've not yet met. I'd like another look round before stepping into the breach. And Daisy—or should I say Sister Marchment?—and I can exchange professional notes,' Adam replied drily, giving Daisy a nod and a tight-lipped smile. A smile, though, she noted, that failed to reach his dark brown eyes, which remained stony and expressionless.

A fresh wave of panic swept over her as her eyes met his. My God, I believe he really hates me, she thought. Will we be able to work together without Matron knowing how he feels about me?

But, whatever the future might hold in store, for the present Matron seemed oblivious of their reaction to each other, and happily ushered them out of her office to start on their round.

Driving away from Featherston Hall through the wet darkness some hours later, Daisy reflected on her peculiar afternoon, which had started so well and ended in a maelstrom of uncertainty.

Her mind seethed with mixed emotions as she recalled what had happened over the last few hours, and especially after Adam had arrived on the scene. Until that moment she had been on a high of excitement, anticipating a wonderful future opening up for her and Rupert, then, quite suddenly, everything had come crashing down about her ears.

Adam so clearly still blamed her for ruining his friend's marriage that she had felt, almost physically, his dislike reaching out to her in Matron's office.

And he had remained aloof, though polite, throughout their tour of the clinic, as Matron, justly proud of her considerable empire, had led them from wing to wing and room to room.

All the while, Daisy had been painfully aware of Adam's strong male presence, and the threat to her peace of mind that he represented. Had he understood her mute message pleading with him not to give away her history? She had been acutely conscious as the afternoon had progressed that he could, by accident or design, at any moment reveal to Matron the fact that she had left her husband before he died, and had not been a grieving young widow. Would he choose to do so? And how would Matron react if he did? Would she accept that this was a piece of information irrelevant to the present situation that Daisy had a right to conceal, or would she feel that she had been deceived, and withdraw the offer of the job?

A cold hand of fear had clutched at her heart as she had considered the possibility. She wanted the job so badly, both for her own and Rupert's sake. And yet, with the possibility of Adam exposing her at any time, did she dare to accept it and live with the threat hanging over her every day? How would this new, mature, more serious Adam, whom she knew nothing about, behave? Would he perhaps see it as a matter of duty, as medical officer, that he should inform Matron of her deception, if he realised that such was the case?

But he hadn't been present at either of her interviews, and didn't know what she had said or not said. For all he knew, she might have told Matron the whole story. Wishful thinking! He was far too perceptive; she was sure that he had guessed at something like the truth. Of course he had, and she had herself tried to convey as much to him in the office so that he wouldn't give her away. Somehow she would have to live with that knowledge.

The tour, which should have been a perfect conclusion to a successful interview, proved to be, due to Adam's presence and the threat he posed, a mixed experience. Daisy had tried to be enthusiastic about all that they saw and to quell her uneasy thoughts.

They had visited each unit in the clinic, from the long-stay medical-rooms, through the mixed acute medical and surgical beds, to the five-bedded maternity unit. They had enthused over the new day-treatment suite, with its small, well-equipped theatre, examination- and recovery-rooms. And although they had both been shown around on previous visits they had been impressed afresh by the brightness and the happy atmosphere that pervaded the clinic. It was homely, in spite of its obvious efficiency, and it was clear that it was all due to Matron Browning's leadership.

Her knowledge and sensitivity to all that was going on was awesome. She seemed to be *au fait* with everything to do with both patients and staff, knowing the most intimate and personal details of both, from medication to whose staff child was about to have a birthday.

If I take the job, thought Daisy, reviewing these events as she drove homewards through the howling wind and rain, she's going to be a hard act to live up to. But I can do that; I'm a good nurse; I can match her. What I'm not sure about is Adam. Can I cope day after day working beside him? Somehow I don't believe that he'll deliberately tell Matron about my small deception, even if he is aware of it. He's too honourable for that, and won't feel that he should interfere. But can he conceal his dislike for me? If he can't, and Matron senses that there's something wrong between us, would she terminate my contract? Yes, she would. Her clinic comes first, and quite right, too; she would do anything to maintain its smooth running.

But surely Adam and I are professional enough to conceal our feelings and work harmoniously together, aren't we? she asked herself. Of course we are. And, though he may never forgive me for leaving Matthew, he'll understand that I want this job for Rupert's sake, and make an effort to be at least superficially friendly.

Questions and answers swirled around in her tormented brain, and then, quite suddenly, her mind cleared and she saw matters from a different aspect. It was going to be all right. Once Adam met Rupert all would be well; she felt certain of it. Adam might continue to dislike her, but he would do all that he could to protect his old friend's son, even going to the lengths of concealing from others his dislike of her, if necessary. Of that she suddenly felt confident. She heaved a great sigh of relief. Her future and Rupert's would be safe at Featherston Hall.

Of course, Adam would be a constant reminder of the poignant part, with its highs and lows. She would never be able to forget the days when she and Adam and Matthew were all young, and she had thought that she was in love with Matthew, and had been, if she was honest, just a little in love with Adam too. If he hadn't gone away, who knew? She might have grown out of her infatuation for Matthew, and what anguish that would have saved her. She might have turned to Adam for comfort. . .even, perhaps, for love.

Turned to Adam!

Her heart gave a little leap at the thought, as a picture of the Adam she had just parted from filled her mind. He had always been a handsome man; now maturity and experience lent distinction to his classic features, the aquiline nose, the firm chin. Now a dusting of grey flecks highlighted his black wiry hair, and a network of fine lines around his eyes enhanced their dark brown depths, while quirky laughter-lines at the corners of his well-shaped mouth emphasised its mobility.

But it hadn't just been Adam's mature good looks that had so impressed her this afternoon; it had been the air of confidence and integrity combined with gentleness emanating from his that she had found so attractive. Everything about him proclaimed him to be a man who could be relied upon at all times; a good doctor. He had an easy yet naturally authoritative way with the patients, which he had, without fuss, demonstrated several times when on the round.

These qualities had come to the fore with one patient in particular, whom he had handled with a nice mixture of firmness and gentleness. She was a young woman expecting her first baby, who had just started an asthma attack as they'd arrived in the luxurious maternity suite.

Matron had put them quickly in the picture, explaining that Mrs Lewis had been admitted two weeks before the end of her pregnancy so that her asthma could be controlled. Apparently, concerned for her baby's safety, she had been trying to avoid using her nebuliser and other medication while at home, or using it very erratically, in spite of being advised otherwise.

'So now it's up to us,' Matron had added in a low voice as they had stood just inside the door, 'to convince Mrs Lewis that her medication is vital to her and the baby, and will not harm the growing foetus.'

'Absolutely essential,' Adam had agreed firmly, moving across the room to the patient's bedside. 'And the sooner the better.'

With a courteous nod to the nurse in attendance, he had sat down on the edge of the bed and introduced himself to the patient. 'I'm Dr Torrence,' he'd said softly. 'Now, let's see what we can do for you, Mrs Lewis, to make you more comfortable.'

Wide-eyed and frightened as she struggled to get her breath, Sarah Lewis had grabbed his hand. 'Help me,' she had gasped between painful, wheezing breaths. 'But don't give me anything that'll hurt my baby.'

'No, we won't do that,' Adam had assured her in his deep, calm voice as he had squeezed her hand and glanced swiftly at the medication lined up on the bedside table. 'Nurse is going to give you a dose of prednisolone, which has been specially prescribed for you. Although it is a powerful steroid and has to be used carefully, it will help and not harm your baby. You are both going to be fine. Just slow down and breathe in quietly. . .and out; that's right, gently does it. . .slow, deep breaths.'

His voice and manner had an almost hypnotic quality, Daisy had thought as she and Matron had stood quietly by, watching him deal with the situation. There had been nothing more they could do. And gradually, as the prednisolone had begun to take effect and Adam's deep, quiet voice succeeded in pacifying and reassuring her, Sarah's breathing had improved and she'd begun to calm down.

It had fortunately been a fairly mild attack, and when she was breathing more or less normally he had examined her thoroughly and had monitored the foetal heart and confirmed that all was well. Then he had explained to her how essential it was for her to continue with her medication. 'It'll be much worse for you and the baby if you don't take whatever treatment is prescribed for you,' he'd said, 'because if you're distressed by enduring an untreated attack, then so is the baby. I want you to promise me that you will take your medicine as necessary from now on,' he had added, smiling down at her flushed face. 'Will you do that?'

Sarah had nodded and produced a tremulous smile in return. 'I will, Doctor, and thank you,' she'd said as they'd left the room.

Matron had looked pleased, and was clearly as impressed as Daisy by Adam's performance and the way he had handled the almost hysterical patient. She had thanked him, and soon after brought the round to an end. They had finished outside theatre, where, operations being over for the day, they had met up with Mr Black, the gynaecological surgeon, and Dr Larry Delaney, the assistant medical officer.

A short while later Daisy had said her goodbyes to the three medicos, deep in conversation, and, having had a few more encouraging words with Matron, had driven away from the elegant, porticoed entrance of Featherston Hall into the blustery, wintry evening.

The weather, she thought now, as she neared the outskirts of the city and the end of her journey, peering through the streaming windows of the car, seemed to match her own chaotic thoughts. What a weird afternoon it had been, with all that had happened, pulling her emotions first one way and then the other.

And now I've got to explain things to Rupert, she reflected. How much do I tell him about meeting up with an old friend of his father's? Will he be pleased, or unaffected by the news, since he doesn't remember Matthew, and only knows that he died when he was a baby? Will it matter to him that I've met up with Adam?

And how does he really feel about moving to the country and away from his school chums? He seemed to be pleased when I told him that I was applying for the job, but was he only pretending to please me, knowing that we've got to make some sort of move? Of course he's missing Aunt Mary; perhaps he'll be glad to get away from the house. He's been so quiet and almost withdrawn since she died. I don't know what he's really thinking any more, poor love.

She hadn't properly marshalled her thoughts when she pulled up outside a neighbour's house, where she had arranged for Rupert to have tea. To her surprise and relief she found that she didn't have to explain anything immediately, for Rupert rushed to the door when she arrived and, giving her a suffocating hug, asked, 'How did it go, Mum; did you get the job?'

'Yes,' she said breathlessly, 'it's mine if I want it.'

'Well, of course you want it,' Rupert said, fixing her with dark brown eyes so like Matthew's. He brushed away his fringe of thick blond hair as he looked up at her. 'Please, Mum, let's go to live in the country. We'll have our own home and you'll be doing the job you want to do, and there'll be plenty of room to play football and ride a bike, and you said there would be other staff kids to play with. . .' His voice trailed off as he looked up at her eagerly.

Daisy's heart contracted as she looked down at Rupert's animated face. She hadn't realised that he'd been so lonely; no wonder he missed Aunt Mary. She said softly, 'We'll talk about it later, love. Fetch your coat, and thank Sue for having you.' She smiled at her friend, Sue Little, and murmured her own thanks as Rupert left the room.

Sue said, 'Think nothing of it; you know I love having him. I just wish I could help you out more often, but unfortunately work doesn't permit it. I'm going to miss you when you move into the wilds of Sussex, but it sounds the right thing for both you and Rupert. He'll meet more kids of his own age there; not many of his friends from school live around here. And the job sounds wonderful—assistant matron; you must be very pleased to be offered the post at your age. You are going to take it, aren't you? You sounded a bit uncertain when you first came in. There aren't any complications, are there?'

'None at all,' said Daisy firmly, squashing the temptation to tell Sue all about Adam, realising that it wouldn't be appropriate. Sue was a good friend, a close one even over the last few years, but at this moment she didn't feel that she could confide in her; everything was too complicated. 'I was just concerned for Rupert that he wouldn't want to leave his friends, but he seems really keen on the idea, doesn't he?'

'He certainly does; he's talked about it almost non-stop this afternoon. To be honest, I think he'll be relieved to change schools. He hasn't said much, but I get the impression that he's not been too happy since he's moved up a class. Did you know that?'

'No, I didn't; he hasn't said a word!' exclaimed Daisy in horrified surprise. 'Oh, why on earth didn't he tell me?'

'He didn't want to worry you, I guess. He's very protective of you, you know, especially since Mary died. What he needs, if you don't mind my saying so, apart from friends of his own age, is a father figure, a sort of role model. And you could do with a man in your life. Do you think you can conjure one up?' she finished with a laugh as Rupert returned to the sitting-room.

Daisy grinned and ignored a picture of Adam which sprang unbidden into her mind's eye. 'Oh, I don't think I'll do anything that drastic,' she said brightly. 'Rupert and I will manage fine together, won't we, love?' She ruffled her son's hair.

'Oh, Mum,' Rupert mumbled as he ducked out from under her hand, his face red with embarrassment at her loving gesture. 'Of course we'll manage,' he said seriously. 'It'll be brilliant if we go to Featherston to live.'

'And that's what we're going home to discuss right now,' said Daisy, giving him a little push towards the door. 'I want to put you fully in the picture before making a final decision.'

A short while later, as she and Rupert sat on the sofa in front of the glowing gas fire in their own sitting-room, Daisy said, in a no-nonsense voice, 'Now, what I want to know is why you didn't tell me that you've been unhappy at school recently.'

Rupert almost choked on a mouthful of Coke. 'Well, I didn't want to worry you, Mum; you've had enough to cope with since Aunt Mary died, what with your work and everything. Anyway, it's nothing. . .'

'What's "nothing"?' Daisy demanded, at once fearful for her son and angry at herself for failing to pick up on this latest problem in her life. 'What's "nothing"?' she repeated more calmly, reminding herself that shouting at Rupert was no solution.

'Well. . .it's just. . .' He faltered for a moment, then told all without hesitation. 'Some of the older boys have been having a go at me. Not badly, Mum, honestly, just stupid stuff. But I can sort it out; you don't have to worry, I know I can handle it.'

'Do you know, I believe you can?' said Daisy, looking into his serious face and steady brown eyes. Eyes that he had inherited from his father, but which tonight reminded her of Adam's enigmatic orbs. 'But you wouldn't mind changing schools, would you?'

'No, that would be great.'

'But it mustn't be your only reason for wanting me to take this job. There might be bullies in any school, you know, even in the small village school at Featherston which you'd be going to. I'll be working long hours, and you'll often have to stay with other people or in the child-minding unit when I'm on duty; will you mind that?'

Rupert gave a little shrug. 'That will happen wherever we go,' he said resignedly, making Daisy's heart turn over, 'but at least at Featherson we'll have our own place, and you'll always be on the spot, even when you're working. I like the idea of living in a bungalow in the grounds, with a big garden round it. Did you see it again today?'

'No, I was too busy looking round the clinic and meeting the new medical officer. And guess what?' She spoke fast and a little breathlessly, her heart in her mouth. How would Rupert take the news? Would he be affected at all? He knew that his father had died when he was about a year old, but he knew nothing about his history. She had always let him think that they'd been together as a family when his father died; there had been no point in telling him the truth. If he ever gave Matthew a thought, she wanted him to believe that his father had been a reliable and loving person.

'What?'

'The new medical officer, Dr Torrence, is an old friend of your father's, and mine too. We were at the same hospital together, years ago.'

'Oh.' Rupert frowned. 'Do you mean you knew him before I was born?'

'Yes.'

'Phew, that's a long time ago. I bet you were surprised to see each other.'

'We were.'

'Were you pleased?'

'Yes,' she said decisively, suddenly realising that in spite of knowing that he would remind her of the good and bad things in her past she was pleased to see Adam again, and looked forward, with reservations, to working with this older, more responsible, intuitive man. If only he felt the same!

'Well, I'm glad for you, Mum,' said Rupert, with a broad smile. 'It'll be much easier for you working with someone you know.' He leaned over and gave her a quick kiss on her cheek. 'I think we're meant to go to Featherston Hall, and you should definitely take the job.'

'Yes, so do I, love. I'll write a letter to Matron tonight.' She gave Rupert a hug. 'Now go and have a bath and get ready for bed while I get some supper ready.'

Rupert had been in bed for some time when the phone rang. Daisy, in the middle of writing her letter of acceptance to Mrs Browning, gave an exasperated sigh, and went out into the hall to answer it. She picked up the receiver, said, 'Good evening,' rather briskly and reeled off her number.

'Ah,' said a deep, familiar voice in her ear. 'Mrs Daisy Marchment, I presume. I've got you at last; you're the fourth D Marchment in the directory that I've rung.'

She almost dropped the receiver. 'Adam,' she said shakily. 'It's you. What are *you* ringing me for?'

'Well, you know, Daisy,' said Adam's disembodied voice, 'I thought that after the trauma of this afternoon, and our unexpected and unwelcome meeting up with each other, *you* might want to talk.'

'T-talk? What about?'

'Well, for starters, about taking up your post here at Featherston now that you know that I'm going to be on the staff; perhaps you're wondering if the place would be big enough for both of us. You seemed to me to be rather distracted when we were doing the round with Matron; I wondered if you might have changed your mind for some reason,' he said flatly.

'Well, I haven't,' she said sharply, in a voice that trembled with anger tinged with fear. How the hell did he know that she very nearly had backed off? Did he have second sight or something? 'Why on earth should I do that?'

'Why, indeed?' he said smoothly. 'Unless you have something to hide.'

To Daisy, at that moment, his smoothness sounded almost menacing. She had been foolish to convince herself that he wouldn't do anything to spoil her chances, once he had got the gist of her unspoken plea this afternoon not to give her away to Matron. Now it looked as if he was going to hold it over her. That was why he wanted to talk to her. She couldn't believe it of him; she felt horribly shocked and disappointed. In a voice a little above a whisper, she asked, 'What should I have to hide?'

He said quietly, reasonably, 'I don't know, Daisy, that's your business, though I can make an educated guess at it. My concern is for Featherston, which is why I want to see you soon and have a chat. I think there's a lot for us to talk about if we're to work together amicably, and that's imperative for the good of the clinic. We owe it to Mrs Browning to sort out a sound working relationship; to work out a set of ground rules, a strategy, even if we can't live up to her expectations of us as old friends reunited, don't you agree?'

Daisy took in a deep breath to calm herself as a wave of relief washed over her. He wasn't going to give her away; he wasn't interested in her secret. She said in a firm voice, 'I couldn't agree more; where shall we meet?'

'I could come to you.'

'No, don't do that,' she said quickly. For some reason she didn't want to meet him in Aunt Mary's house, which had for so long been her home. She preferred to see him on neutral ground, make a fresh start.

'All right, then let's meet at a village called Kingsfield just south of Crawley; that's about halfway between here and London. There's a nice pub in the high street that I went to with friends recently; it's called Pilgrims. It's an old coaching inn and there's plenty of parking space in the yard behind, so you shouldn't have any problems on that score. We could meet for lunch. Do you think you can make it some time next week, or the week after?'

'Yes, I can take a day off Tuesday week. Rupert will be at school, so lunchtime will be perfect.'

'Twelve-thirty suit you?'

'Fine. It's a date.'

'A business date,' he reminded her in cool tones, 'to iron out any difficulties that might arise in the future, nothing more.'

Furious that he had lulled her almost into a false sense of security, Daisy said angrily, 'Don't worry, Adam Torrence, I wouldn't want anything but a *business* date with you. Goodnight.'

She slammed the phone down and stood staring at it for a few moments, her chest heaving as she drew in several deep, painful breaths. How dared he lead her on and make her feel safe and then remind her that he was only seeing her for the sake of the clinic?

All her previous doubts about taking the job at Featherston Hall and working with Adam rose to the surface. It just wasn't possible; one way or another he was going to make life difficult for her. She had better write to Matron and turn down the job and somehow explain her change of mind to Rupert.

She could have wept. If only Aunt Mary were here so that she could confide in her. But then the situation would never have arisen. She clenched her hands in anger and frustration and near despair, and brushed at the tears that trickled down her face.

The stairs creaked, and she looked up to see Rupert looking sleepily down at her from the top stair.

'Mum, are you all right?' he asked. 'I heard the phone. Why are you crying?'

'I'm not crying, I've got something in my eye,' she lied, hoping he couldn't see her too plainly in the dimmish hall light. 'And it was only somebody from the hospital on the phone—you know, the usual problems about off duty.'

'You sounded very cross.'

'Well, some people are impossible and unreasonable,' she told him as casually as she could.

'Never mind, it'll be better when we move to the clinic at Featherston. I bet you won't have as many problems there—it's going to be brilliant.'

'No, I don't suppose I will,' she said with quiet resignation, knowing at that moment that she would finish her letter of acceptance to Matron and meet Adam as arranged. No way was she going to jeopardise her son's future because she hadn't the courage to face up to problems. 'Goodnight, darling, sleep well.'

'Goodnight, Mum,' said Rupert as he turned and made his way back to his room.

CHAPTER THREE

FOR Daisy the days between her telephone conversation with Adam and her meeting with him at the pub in Kingsfield passed swiftly. Although she was very busy preparing for her move to Featherston, as well as working out her notice at the hospital, Adam was frequently in her thoughts. She found that though one part of her dreaded meeting him again, or rather dreaded what he might be going to say, another part of her was intrigued by the thought of seeing the new, mature Adam.

Surprisingly, it was not the cold, distant Adam Torrence who still seemed to despise her whom she saw in her mind's eye; it was the warm, compassionate doctor who had attended the pregnant asthmatic young woman who came sharply into focus. If only he would show that gentle side of his nature to her, she thought sadly. If only he would believe, even after all these years, her version of the events that had led up to her leaving Matthew, he might cease to dislike her as intensely as he seemed to do.

If only. . . Oh, hell. Well, perhaps over the next few months, or even years if they continued to work together, she could put matters straight. She would certainly do her damnedest. For some obscure reason she wanted his respect, even if she couldn't have his friendship, otherwise life at Featherston would never be truly fulfilling. It would be flawed.

So it had been with mixed feelings that she had sent

off her letter of acceptance to Matron Browning, and her letter of resignation to the administrators of the trust hospital for whom she presently worked. She had sighed with a kind of resigned relief when she had done so, for there was no turning back now—she was committed.

But one person at least had no doubts about their future at Featherston. Rupert was looking forward to the move with undiluted happiness, and that comforted Daily immensely. It made her even more determined to make a success of her new job and come to terms with working with Adam, however difficult that might be. Even her forthcoming meeting with the doctor won Rupert's approval. She had worried that it might be difficult explaining to him why she was meeting Adam before taking up her post at the clinic, fearing that her son might ask awkward questions that she couldn't answer honestly. But her fears had been unfounded. It seemed that anything to do with their new life had his approbation.

'Course you want to see him,' he'd said, when she'd rather tentatively told him that she was meeting Adam. 'I expect you have a lot to talk about, being old friends.' And as she dropped him off at school on the morning of her meeting with Adam he said cheerfully, 'Have a nice day, Mum, with Dr Torrence. See you at teatime.'

Daisy remembered Rupert's words when a couple of hours later she drove through the quiet country lanes of Sussex to Kingsfield. If only it *were* a meeting to reminisce about old times instead of a formal get-together to discuss future strategy! How cold and unfriendly that sounded—'future strategy'. It was almost like planning a war—a cold war. In spite of the warmth of the car and her thick, baggy woollen sweater and warm trousers she shivered, and her heart seemed to chill at the thought.

She found Pilgrims without any difficulty, just as Adam had described it, about halfway down the steep high street that ran through the village. Although it was nearly twelve-thirty the large cobbled yard at the rear of the ancient coaching inn was still covered in thick frost that glittered in the pale wintry sunshine. There were a dozen or so cars already parked there, but she had no difficulty in finding space for her small Fiat, slotting in between a chunky, powerful-looking Range Rover and a sleek-looking red Porsche. Fleetingly, she wondered if the Porsche belonged to Adam, for the showy vehicle would certainly have suited the Adam she used to know. Were his tastes still the same? she wondered.

There was so much, she thought, as she made her way carefully over the slippery, frosted cobbles to the rear door of the inn, that she didn't know about the new Adam. Would she discover more about him today?

A small flight of steps led down into the lounge bar of the inn, and for a few moments Daisy stood at the top of them looking down into the smoky, dim interior, trying to locate him. For some reason she was sure that he would already be there waiting for her, and suddenly there he was, looking up at her from the foot of the stairs.

His strong, aquiline features were thrown into relief by the rosy glow from the wall lamps and the leaping flames of the wood fire behind him. The subdued lighting emphasised his height and the breadth of his wide shoulders. Her heart gave a little leap of excitement. He looked incredibly handsome and so solidly reassuring. Surely everything was going to be all right? she thought; she couldn't possibly remain enemies with this large, confident-looking man.

It was a disappointment that he greeted her coolly, with a nod and an expressionless, 'Good afternoon.'

'Hello,' she said rather breathlessly as she moved down the stairs. 'I hope I haven't kept you waiting.'

'Not at all; it's only just twelve-thirty,' he drawled in his deep voice. 'But you always were a good timekeeper, Daisy, as I remember.'

'Was I?'

'Yes,' he said quietly, 'you were.' He was still unsmiling—in fact his face looked stern—but she fancied that there was a hint of warmth now in his voice.

She stumbled on the last step, and he put out a hand to steady her. To her annoyance, his touch made her tremble and, hoping that he hadn't noticed, she quickly pulled her arm free from his light grasp.

'Thank you, I can manage,' she said stiffly, inwardly cursing her stiffness.

He rasied his eyebrows and allowed himself a small, lop-sided smile. 'Oh, I'm sure you can,' he replied evenly, looking down at her, a cool, appraising expression in his eyes.

She stared back at him and felt her cheeks glow. How *could* he be so calm? It wasn't fair. Obviously he was not as affected by their meeting as she was. Or was he much better at concealing his feelings? What feelings? He disliked and despised her because of what he imagined she had done to his precious friend Matthew; those were his only feelings for her; he had made that plain.

She stood at the bottom of the steps, her eyes locked on to his. If only he could like her a little!

It was as if he had read that last thought in her eyes, and for a moment felt compassion, even sympathy for her. For the look in his own eyes, from being appraising, changed, warmed, softened.

Daisy's heartbeats quickened as the realisation came to her that, at least for the moment, he didn't seem to despise her. It was incredible; perhaps she had made a breakthrough. She lowered her eyes so that he shouldn't see the hope that flared in them. She must play it cool, not seem too eager, or he would back off.

He said softly, 'Come, let's sit by the fire; you look as if you could do with warming up.' He turned and led the way round other tables and chairs to the massive fireplace at the end of the room. He guided her into an oak settle to one side of the blazing log fire. 'Now, what'll you have to drink?'

'A tomato juice, please.'

'Not very warming; somehow I thought you might be a dry-sherry lady these days, very smooth and sophisticated.'

Was he being sarcastic? No, of course not! Why should he be? He had simply made a perfectly innocuous remark. She mustn't read alternative meanings into everything he said. Mustn't let him rattle her.

'I'm driving, and I never drink when I drive,' she replied.

'Really? How very sensible,' he said drily, and to her taut senses it sounded as if he was rather surprised by her responsible attitude and was teasing her about it. 'You won't condemn me, though, will you, if I have half a real ale before eating; it won't offend your principles in any way?'

His voice gave nothing away, and yet again she wondered if he was being sarcastic, or just trying to needle her. Surely not, not this new, responsible Adam? She couldn't believe that he would condone drinking and driving, or make fun of her because she felt strongly about it. She realised that because she was nervous she *was* reading all sorts of meanings into everything he said.

She looked up at him and smiled. 'Of course not; I'm sure you wouldn't dream of going over the limit, and for a man of your size half a pint is quite acceptable.'

'Indeed it is, and you're right, I wouldn't consider touching the limit.' He looked at her for a moment with dark, serious eyes, then stood up abruptly. 'I'll fetch our drinks,' he said, moving towards the bar.

Daisy was thoughtful as she watched him go. She knew so little about this new Adam, she found it difficult to assess him. She wasn't even sure why he had wanted to see her. If it was simply to know what she had told Matron when she'd applied for the job, why not say so, why not ask her over the phone? Anyway, he had said when he'd telephoned her that he wasn't interested in her past, or how she had presented herself to Matron, only in the future. Had he changed his mind? Was he going to warn her that he would expose her unless she fell in with whatever he suggested? No, somehow, as she had already decided, she couldn't see him doing that. It would be a kind of blackmail, and he wouldn't stoop to that.

A thought suddenly struck her that made her draw in her breath sharply. Had he something to hide himself, or someone to protect from the past that he thought she might know about? Not likely, but possible. Hard on its heels came another thought. Was Adam married, or did he have a partner, or was he divorced? She didn't think he was married, for almost certainly Matron would have mentioned it, if only casually. But a partner, yes, or divorced, yes, both strong possibilities. But neither would have presented him with any real problems. He would not have allowed either contingency to present him with difficulties when applying for the post of medical officer at Featherston. She didn't doubt that his medical qualifications, references and experience were first-class and he would have secured the job on those alone.

She was still deep in thought when he arrived back with their drinks. He sat down beside her on the cushioned settle and picked up his glass and saluted her with it before taking a large swallow. 'Reached any conclusions about me?' he asked drily, almost taking her breath away with his directness.

He gave her a long, hard, challenging look from his dark, enigmatic brown eyes. She picked up her own glass and took a sip of tomato juice, then lifted her chin defiantly and met his gaze. 'There speaks the true egotist,' she said, with a rather forced little laugh. 'Why are you so sure that I was thinking of you?'

'Well, I would be in your place,' he said calmly, continuing to look her straight in the eye. 'Quite naturally you're curious about me after all these years. Am I married or do I have a partner? Have I been divorced half a dozen times?'

'And have you. . .are you married, divorced or living with someone?'

Daisy thought that she saw a bleak look come into his eyes for a moment, but he smiled as he said, 'No, I don't fit into any of those categories, thought I had a steady relationship with someone for a couple of years.'

It occurred to her that if he had tried living with someone he must know how hard it was to sustain a relationship, and shouldn't judge her too harshly. Perhaps after all she could make him understand why she had left Matthew. 'Really? What happened? Did she walk out on you or you on her?' she asked in a cool, faintly sarcastic voice.

'Neither. We kept faith with each other, although we weren't married. Kate died rather slowly of a tropical fever, when we were working in Africa.'

Feeling desperately ashamed of her sarcasm, Daisy turned a stricken face towards him, sympathy swamping every other emotion. 'Oh, Adam, I *am* sorry; how dreadful for you.' She put her hand on his sleeve.

'Yes, it was pretty grim, but at least we were together.' He looked down at her hand with a frown and gently but firmly removed it from his arm. The gesture of rejection was like a slap in the face. It seemed that he didn't want anything from her, not even her sympathy. 'And I suppose,' he said in a strained voice, 'that in that respect we were luckier than many—being together to the very end.'

The reference to her and Matthew was obvious, because they hadn't been together when Matthew died. But she squashed the angry desire to rush to her own defence, realising that Adam must still be badly hurt by what had happened, and was lashing out at her to relieve his feelings. It struck her that perhaps it was partly on account of his personal tragic experience that he continued to feel so bitter about her and Matthew. She said softly, 'You must have been madly in love with Kate.'

To her surprise, he shook his head and responded quietly, 'No, we never pretended to be the world's greatest lovers. We both had people in our past and were honest about it and loved and respected each other, but were not in love.' He shrugged his broad shoulders. 'We were lonely. I suppose you might say that we comforted each other, strangers in a strange land, both grieving for something that might have been.'

Daisy's tender heart turned over and her eyes glistened with unshed tears. 'Oh, Adam, I'm so very sorry,' she whispered.

He gave her a long, hard look and said harshly, 'Yes, I believe you are, but what a pity you——'

He broke off as the bell that was normally rung to call time clanged loudly, and everyone turned to look in surprise towards the bar. The barman called out, ''Scuse me, ladies and gentlemen, but there's been a bit of an accident in the cellar. We're gonna need a bit of help. Is anyone a first-aider or something? It's quite urgent.'

None of the customers moved or spoke.

Adam swore under his breath and said savagely, 'That's all we need; so much for our quiet luncheon.' He sighed. 'I'm sorry about this, but we'd better own up; duty calls.'

Daisy's face was pale and set. 'Yes,' she said quietly, 'we'd better.' Heart pounding, in a daze, trying to forget his last bitter, accusing words, she followed him to the bar. What had he been going to accuse her of when he had been interrupted? His eyes had again been as hard and cold as when they had first met. Perhaps now she would never know; by the time they had dealt with the accident, he might have forgotten. No, she thought sadly, he would never forget, but would he ever forgive?

She was brought back to earth with a jolt as she heard

Adam speaking to the barman, explaining who they were.

The barman said, 'Thank God, a doctor *and* a nurse.' He lifted a flap in the counter so that they could pass through, and opened a door at the rear of the bar. He led them into a short corridor with another door, and steps leading off to one side. 'You go down the steps to the cellar,' he directed, standing back to let them pass. 'The boss is down there with our cellarman and the delivery bloke. They're both hurt, but I don't know how badly. When we heard the racket the boss went down to see what it was all about, then he called up to say that there'd been accident and Trev's legs were squashed and to get help, that's all.'

He shrugged nervously. 'Look, I'm not much good at this sort of thing. To tell you the truth I'm a bit squeamish about blood and that. I'd better leave you to it and get back to the bar where I can be useful, unless you really need me to help; I'll do what I can if I have to.'

'For a start you can ring for an ambulance,' said Adam. 'It sounds as if we're going to need one. Better be safe than sorry.'

'OK, will do,' replied the barman, turning away with obvious relief and hurrying back towards the bar, leaving them standing at the top of the stairs.

'Well, at least he's honest,' said Adam, with a shrug, 'and knows his limitations.'

Daisy nodded. 'Yes, poor man, he looked really shaken, but then, even when you're used to it, accidents can be grim to cope with.'

'True,' replied Adam as they started down the stone steps. 'Be careful,' he added as they descended, taking her arm in a firm grip. 'They look rather slippery.'

'Yes, they do,' she replied, very conscious of, and welcoming, his strong, supportive hand. A wave of regret washed over her. Why couldn't he be like this all the time, friendly and concerned, instead of cold and hostile? His manner was quite different now compared to what it had been minutes before when they were having their drinks. It seemed that only a medical emergency could wipe away his intense dislike of her. She felt prickly, apprehensive about what the future might bring. She shivered at the thought.

Adam misinterpreted her reaction. He seemed to think that it had to do with what they might find in the cellar. 'Don't worry,' he said, smiling down at her and giving her arm a gentle squeeze. 'You'll be all right once you start doing something useful. The old adrenalin will start pumping around.'

'Of course I'll be fine.'

They rounded a bend in the stairs and the cellar came fully into view. For some reason Daisy had expected that it would be dim, but in fact it was brightly lit by several high-powered strip-lights and also by an oblong of daylight from the pavement above, where the hatchway to the delivery chute remained open. They paused for a brief moment as they looked down on the scene below them. Halfway down the chute, lying very flat on his back, was a man with a trickle of blood coming from a cut in his temple. Near the foot of the chute a large metal beer barrel had come to rest and a little to one side of it lay another man, groaning, and obviously in pain. Kneeling beside him was a third man.

The kneeling man, whom they took to be the landlord, looked up as Adam and Daisy descended the last few steps. 'Thanks for coming,' he said in a relieved voice. 'I hope you can help. Either of you medical?' he asked hopefully.

'Yes, I'm a doctor and this lady's a nurse,' Adam replied in his calm, unruffled manner as he moved swiftly across the cellar. He turned to Daisy. 'You check out the chap on the chute,' he said quietly, 'while I see what I can do here.' He squatted on his heels beside the injured man and felt for his pulse. 'What's his name?' he asked the landlord.

'Trevor.'

'Trevor, I'm a doctor—Adam Torrence. Can you hear me?'

'Yeah.' The man's eyes flickered open and focused on Adam, who automatically noted that the pupils looked equal and quite normal, though without a proper examination he couldn't be a hundred per cent sure.

He asked in a quiet, reassuring voice, 'Can you tell me where it hurts most, Trevor, apart from your legs? I can see that they're in a mess, but did you hurt yourself anywhere else when you fell?'

'I don't think so. My head feels a bit sore. I hit the ground bloody hard when I fell backwards. Pete, the silly sod, tried to save the barrel when he slipped, and sent it sideways off the chute, knocking me off my feet.' His face was screwed up with pain as he gasped out, 'Doc, my legs hurt like hell; are they broken?'

'I'm not sure, old chap; it certainly looks as if one of them is. I'll take a proper look at them in a minute, and give you something to help the pain while we're waiting for the ambulance,' Adam explained. He fished a key from his pocket and proffered it to the landlord. 'Will you do something for me, please? Fetch my surgical case from the back of my car. It's tucked under the seat in the dark blue Range Rover in the corner of the yard.'

'At once, Doctor.' The landlord took the key and bounded up the steps, clearly pleased to have something practical to do.

Daisy finished her external examination of the other injured man, and moved over to crouch down beside Adam.

'I've checked him over,' she said softly. 'The cut on his temple is superficial, but he is concussed, though not deeply. He was able to tell me that his name is Pete, and he's forty-five. But he can't remember clearly how he fell. He opened his eyes on command, and his pupils look slightly unequal. His pulse is rapid and weak, and he's pale and sweaty, and he's lying awkwardly. I'm not happy about his back, or the possibility of internal or head injuries.'

'Doesn't sound too good; better not move him unless he starts to vomit,' Adam murmured with a frown. He stood up and moved a step backwards and motioned Daisy to do the same so that Trevor could not hear what was said. 'You stay here with Trevor for a minute and I'll have a look at Pete. When the landlord gets back we'll get him to organise some blankets and close that trapdoor up there; at least we can keep these chaps warm. There's not a lot else we can do for Pete, but we can give Trevor a shot of morphine and take a better look at his legs. Poor chap, from what I can see I'm pretty sure that he's got a below-knee fracture, probably his right tib and fib.'

His eyes met Daisy's for a moment, and they looked neither hostile nor cold, just rather serious and concerned. To her surprise, he reached out and squeezed her hand. 'Sorry about all this,' he said. 'I'm afraid our lunch is virtually a write-off; it'll be a ploughman's at the bar if we're lucky.'

'Not to worry; that suits me. I have to be back to meet Rupert from school by just after three and it's nearly an hour's drive.'

'Understood,' said Adam as he moved towards the injured man on the chute. 'Don't worry, I'll make sure that you get away in good time.'

A few moments later, while Adam was still examining the possibly seriously injured Pete, and Daisy was reassuring Trevor, the landlord arrived with Adam's surgical case. 'Is there anything else I can do?' he asked as he handed it over.

'Yes,' said Adam. 'You can get that delivery hatch closed and get some blankets down here to cover these men with. We've got to do our best to keep them warm till the ambulance comes.'

They had to wait for some time for the ambulance to arrive. When it came, the driver and paramedic on board were apologetic. They had been flagged down by the police to attend a minor traffic accident and no other ambulance had been available.

While they had been waiting for the ambulance Adam had given Trevor a pain-killing injection of morphine, and, with Daisy's expert help, attended to his legs. They had cut away his trousers and put clean, dry dressings over the open wounds on both legs, and then applied makeshift splints to the broken leg.

They had not been able to do much for Pete, who had remained in a dazed though not deeply unconscious state. They had covered him with a blanket, constantly reassured him, and had taken his pulse at regular intervals and observed other vital signs. The chance of him having a depressed skull fracture because he had landed hard on the back of his head was high. There was nothing else they could do; he needed all the high-powered treatment that a hospital intensive-care unit could give him.

It was twenty to two when they returned to the bar. A grateful landlord hovered round them offering food and drink on the house. But they refused everything but a ploughman's and coffee.

While they waited for their meal they speculated with professional and concerned interest on the fate of their two patients. Had they done all they could for them and how would they do? Would they make a speedy recovery? Was Pete suffering from a depressed fracture of the skull, as his unequal pupils seemed to indicate, or was it something less serious? Would Trevor's badly smashed right leg mend satisfactorily?

Their original reason for meeting in the pub faded into the background during the course of their animated professional discussion, and when their meal arrived they ate and drank in companionable silence. To Daisy's surprise she discovered that she was hungry and attacked her Stilton and crusty rolls with relish. She glanced at the clock over the bar as she finished—it was just past two o'clock.

'Adam, I'm sorry but. . .'

'I know, you've got to go; understood. You mustn't be late picking the boy up from school.' He stretched a hand out to cover hers and surprised her by asking in a low, gentle voice, 'Is Rupert anything like Matthew?'

He really wanted to know.

After a moment's hesitation, she said, 'Well, his eyes are dark brown like Matthew's were, and he's got his nose, but otherwise he's rather like me. He's got blond hair like mine; it looks great with his brown eyes and. . .' Adam was staring at her with his own enigmatic dark brown eyes that gave nothing away. She wasn't even sure that he was listening.

He said suddenly, harshly, squeezing her hand hard as he did so, making her wince with pain, 'Why the hell did you walk out on Matthew, Daisy? He loved you and the boy so much. How could you do it to him?'

His words and tone shocked her. She pulled her hand from beneath his. Her heart felt like lead; she couldn't believe this was happening now, not after they had just worked together, eaten together, so amicably, so harmoniously. With an effort she said calmly, 'I tried to tell you when you were on leave; Matthew was a drunk, a womaniser, and had a violent temper. But you didn't listen, and he covered his tracks well. He didn't want me, except as someone to fall back on when he was in difficulties, and I couldn't risk him hurting Rupert.'

'Matthew was never like that! He could be a bit wild at times, but all he needed was your support and you let him down; all that "till death us do part" didn't mean anything to you,' Adam said in a hard, cold voice.

'Yes, it did, and I didn't let him down! He went further downhill after you went abroad again; he cheated on me many times before Rupert was born. I tried to make things work. . .' She swallowed and her eyes glistened, on the brink of shedding tears. If only she could make him understand. But it was no good. She could see by the look on his face that he didn't believe her.

Adam said in a level voice, 'I wish I could believe you, Daisy, but I can't. If only you could be honest with me, trust me with the truth, I might at least understand why you acted as you did. After all, you can fall out of love as well as into it. I can appreciate that. But you persist in making Matthew out to be some kind of monster who was a threat to you and your son, and salve your conscience by putting the blame on him. I don't believe that the Matthew I knew could have turned out like that. No, as he told me, you left him for somebody else, and since you still pose as Mrs Marchment I can only presume that you later left the other man too.'

Daisy knew then, looking at Adam's hard, handsome face, with its formidable nose and deep-set eyes, that she was defeated. She would never be able to make him see Matthew as he really had been in those last few years, when the dashing streak in him had grown to a violent one. All Adam could see was the attractive, full-of-fun person who had been his friend through student and early medical days. He couldn't, or wouldn't, believe anything ill of him.

Just as he hadn't believed her side of the story all those years ago, when he had come back from abroad and pleaded with her on Matthew's behalf. If he hadn't believed her then, why should she think that he would believe her now?

She felt drained, exhausted, almost beyond tears; there was nothing else she could say. To think that this clever, dedicated doctor sitting next to her, who was so perceptive about his patients and other people, could be so blind to her situation, so unreasonable. She looked at her watch—nearly ten past two.

Wearily she gathered up her shoulder-bag, and said in a toneless voice, 'I have to go now, Adam. Thank you for my lunch. I'm afraid we haven't got very far with our strategy for our future at the clinic, but I'll go along with whatever you devise, as long as you do nothing to hurt Rupert.'

In a flash, Adam snaked out a hand, put a finger under her chin and tilted her head so that she was forced to meet his eyes with her own. He said softly, 'My God, Daisy, do you really think that I would do anything to harm Matthew's boy, however strongly I feel about you and your deception? Don't worry, your secret's safe with me. Matron can go on believing you to be a grieving young widow forever, as far as I'm concerned. Neither by word nor action will she learn differently from me. And, far from hurting Rupert, I hope that I might get to know him better. Who knows? He might even grow to like and trust me, unlike his mother, as time goes by.'

Trying to keep a hold on her emotions, Daisy drove up the A23 to London and the school to collect Rupert. Her mind circled round the events of the afternoon, from the time she had met Adam, through the medical emergency, to when she had left him a while ago. So much had been compressed into that hour and a half. Adam's reaction to her had wavered up and down like a barometer in free fall.

He had been distant but polite when they'd first met, warm and friendly and caring when they'd been attending the injured men in the cellar, treating her as a valued colleague, and downright cold and unkind just before they'd parted. Who was the true Adam Torrence—image one, two or three? Or was he just variable where she was concered? All she was sure about as she drove through the pale sunshine of the February afternoon was that if it had not been for Rupert she would have backed off from working at

Featherston Hall. The joy of taking the assistant matron's post was wiped out by Adam's presence.

How cruel fate was, bringing them together in a small downland village where they would be working closely together, when they might have passed like ships in the night in any vast city hospital.

But she would have to pretend for Rupert's sake. He must not have any idea how much she dreaded taking up her new appointment. No way must she diminish his enthusiasm for living in the country. He was so looking forward to having a bike and being able to use it safely in the grounds of the clinic; and he was looking forward to changing schools. Perhaps, too, he wanted to get away from memories of Aunt Mary, who had played such a big part in his young life. Who could appreciate the emotional values and needs of a child of eight?

She arrived at the school and sat in the car waiting for Rupert to come out. With a pang, she realised that she didn't know any of the other mothers waiting by the gates. Except on rare occasions, Aunt Mary had always collected Rupert. No wonder he missed her.

There was no doubt about it; the sooner they moved to Featherston for his benefit the better.

Resolutely she turned a smiling face to meet her son when he emerged through the school gates.

'Did you have a nice day, Mum,' he asked as he fastened his seatbelt, 'talking about olden times with old Dr Torrence?'

'Do you mind?' said Daisy, her voice heavy with sarcasm. 'Not so much of the "olden" or the "old"; he's not Methuselah, you know.'

'Who's Methuselah?'

'A very wise old man who lived a long time ago and died at a great age.'

'Oh, I see. Well, anyway, did you have a nice day talking to Dr Torrence?'

'Yes,' said Daisy, lying through her teeth, 'I did.'

'Oh, good. Mum, can I have pizza and baked beans for tea?'

'Of course you can, darling,' said Daisy.

CHAPTER FOUR

DAISY wondered if Adam would try to get in touch with her again after their abortive and unhappy meeting in the pub, but he didn't. She felt so battered and mixed up by the whole business that she didn't know whether to be glad or sorry that he was silent. Sometimes she felt that if they did meet again she would be able to win him over; at other times she despaired of ever doing so. Their reaction to each other had see-sawed over several layers of emotion.

But there was one faint glimmer of hope, she reminded herself; Adam had made it abundantly clear that he would never do anything to spoil Rupert's future; in fact, quite the opposite. That at least was a comfort. It meant that if she could stand the tension of working with him her job was safe.

With enormous self-control she kept her feelings hidden from Rupert, who was enthusiastically counting off the days to their move.

Towards the end of February, on a wet, bleak day, she and Rupert went over to Featherston, at Matron's invitation, to look round the bungalow that was to be their home.

Although Daisy had tried to describe Featherston Hall to him, Rupert was surprised and a little bit awed by the size of the clinic and the outlying buildings, standing high on the hillside, clearly visible between the bare trees from the lane, as they approached.

There was nothing much left of the original gracious

eighteenth-century mansion except the porticoed entrance and the reception hall and the two lodges at the foot of the drive. For Featherston Hall, almost in its entirety, had been burnt down in the thirties and a modern building, all glass and white walls and rounded turrets to make the most of the sun, had been built in its place. In the seventies this had been enlarged in similar style by Mrs Browning and her husband; they had added several wings to the building to house the present clinic. They had also added staff quarters, a small operating theatre, and a centre for minor surgery. And there was a health-cum-leisure centre, complete with sauna, squash court and swimming-pool.

'Wow! Isn't it something?' Rupert exclaimed, staring wide-eyed at the large cluster of buildings on the hillside. And he was further intrigued when a few minutes later he saw the two eighteenth-century lodges, built like miniature castles, one at either side of the drive. 'Who lives in those, Mum?' he asked as they drove past.

'Matron, Mrs Browning, lives in one, and Dr Torrence in the other,' she replied, her voice involuntarily tightening a little as she said Adam's name.

They continued up the twisting drive until they rounded a bend and Featherston Hall loomed up before them in all its impressive glory.

'It's enormous,' said Rupert as he surveyed the building at close quarters.

'Not really,' said Daisy with a laugh as she stopped on the wide sweep of gravel by the front entrance. 'It's nothing like the size of a city hospital. It's just that it's rather spread out, being on only three floors. And, of course, there are all the outbuildings. Now let's go and introduce you to Matron, and collect the key to our bungalow.'

Matron welcomed them warmly, shook Rupert's hand and had a few minutes' interesting, non-patronising conversation with him. They took to each other at once.

Handing over the key to the bungalow, Matron said matter-of-factly, 'As you know, Daisy, it's partly furnished at the moment, but we can store whatever you don't want to use, or let you have more furniture if you need it.'

'We've got some things which my aunt left us,' Daisy explained. 'And some bits and pieces that we've collected over the years. I think we'll have enough to furnish it completely.'

'Splendid. It's so much nicer to have your own things around you; makes it really home. Just let me know what you want removed and I'll make the necessary arrangements. When you've finished looking round come back and have some tea and another chat.'

The staff houses and bungalows were separated from the clinic buildings by a sloping field, where some horses were grazing, and a small copse of trees. They were reached by a hard-surfaced lane branching off from the main drive at right angles along the side of the hill. The staff complex was within easy walking distance of the main building, but as it was still pouring with rain they used the car.

Rupert said as he scrambled into the passenger seat, 'Mrs Browning's nice, Mum, isn't she? Not a bit what I expected. I was a bit scared of meeting her.'

'She's stunning,' replied Daisy, giving him a smile as she reflected how well he had risen to the occasion, being polite but chatty in the nicest possible way. She was proud of him.

The bungalow was one of a dozen or more mixed houses and bungalows built round a central green called The Close. Rupert was thrilled with their neat, detached bungalow.

'It's brill, Mum, just like you said!' he exclaimed excitedly as they finished their inspection of the two good-sized bedrooms, large living-room and well-equipped kitchen and bathroom. And he was even more thrilled with the fair-sized integral garage-cum-workshop. 'There'll be plenty of room for my bike in the garage as well as the car,' he said happily.

'*When* you get a bike,' said Daisy with a laugh.

'Oh, Mum, you *promised* I'd have one when we moved to the country,' Rupert wailed in an anguished voice.

'It's all right, love, I was only teasing. Of course you'll have a bike, but not immediately. Give me a week or two to get over the move.'

'Couldn't we get it before we move?' he asked hopefully.

'Not a chance,' Daisy told him in the firm voice that Rupert knew brooked no argument. 'We'll go into Brighthelm to buy one once we're settled in. And I'm glad that you like the bungalow; it'll look even better when we get our own furniture in,' she said, trying to sound enthusiastic for her son's sake. For him it was a great adventure, and he must never know with what mixed feelings she anticipated living at Featherston and working daily with Adam Torrence. He must believe her to be as excited at the prospect as he was. 'And it's nicely carpeted and curtained, isn't it?' she added tentatively, not quite certain how interested he would be in such basic matters.

'Yeah,' he said, looking round carefully. 'I like the colours, all browns and oranges. And I like the garden too—it's huge, and the path goes all round the side of the bungalow so I'll be able to skateboard. And there are some kids living next door, 'cos I can see a swing and a slide in the back garden. And, Mum, do you think the children living here are allowed to play on the green in the middle?'

'I'm sure they are. Matron said something about football and stoolball and cricket being played there.'

'Mega!'

'Now come and look at the bedrooms again,' said Daisy, putting an arm round his shoulders, noting with a pang how much he had grown recently, 'and tell me which one you would like.'

He didn't hesitate. 'The corner one that looks out over the lane on one side and the fields at the back; that's the one I'd like.'

'Then it's yours,' said Daisy. 'I'm quite happy with the one next door to the bathroom that looks out over the garden and fields at the back.'

'You're sure, Mum?' Rupert asked anxiously.

'Positive.'

'Brilliant!' he exclaimed, giving her a hug. 'It's going to be great living here, isn't it?' His large, luminous brown eyes looked suddenly serious, his voice telling her that he needed reassurance. He was, after all, for all his grown-up approach to the move, only eight.

'Yes,' said Daisy, making a valiant effort to squash all her doubts, 'it is.'

They smiled at each other, and at that moment the front doorbell rang.

'Now who on earth can that be?' exclaimed Daisy in surprise.

'Well, there's one way to find out, Mum,' said Rupert, his confidence restored, his smile widening to a cheeky grin. 'I'll go and open the door and see. I bet it's one of our new neighbours come to say hello,' he added eagerly. 'Wouldn't that be great?'

'Yes, it's probably a colleague or a neighbour come to welcome us,' said Daisy. 'I'd better go.' But her voice fell on deaf ears as Rupert rushed eagerly out of the room and down the passage, his feet, in their rubber-soled trainers, clumping softly on the parquet floor. She stifled a sigh as she followed him to the front door. He was so looking forward to living in Featherston; she just prayed that he wouldn't be hurt or disappointed by the reality.

Rupert swung the door open and Daisy, standing behind him, put an involuntary hand to her throat as she saw who was standing in the porch. It was Adam Torrence. She stood as still as a statue as her astonished eyes met his over her son's head. He was the last person she had expected to see. How did he know she was here? Why had he come?

She stared speechlessly at him for a moment, and before she had recovered herself Rupert asked happily, beaming with pleasure, 'Hello, are you one of our neighbours, or one of Mum's new colleagues?'

Adam smiled down at Rupert. 'Both,' he said, 'though I don't live in The Close but down at the bottom of the drive. I'm also an old friend of your mother's.'

'Do you live in one of the little castles by the gates?'

'I do.'

'Then you're Dr Torrence,' said Rupert triumphantly, 'and you knew my mum and dad before I was born. Mum told me all about you.'

Adam gave a throaty chuckle. 'Did she, indeed? Nothing bad, I hope?'

'Nope, just nice things,' said Rupert, with another beaming smile.

'And you're Rupert; she told me all about you too.' He took Rupert's small hand in his large one and shook it formally.

'Did she?' said Rupert, and added naughtily, mimicking Adam, 'Just nice things I hope, Dr Torrence?'

'You bet—the best,' said Adam with a laugh.

Daisy at last found her tongue. She felt ruffled and angry with Adam for catching her unawares, but did her best to hide it. 'Do come in, Adam,' she said, trying to inject a little warmth into her voice, 'but I'm afraid I've nothing to offer you, not even tea or coffee; the larder's quite bare. We're only here on a flying visit to look around before moving in next week.'

'Yes, so Matron said.' His eyes met hers again as he stepped into the small hall. They were unreadable, yet only moments before when he had been talking to Rupert they had been full of light and laughter. 'But I can't stay; I've a list of patients to see in the day clinic— you know, check-ups and new admissions and so on. We're terribly busy; we could do with your help right now. Believe me, you'll be greeted with open arms when you start work. I just called in to meet Rupert and say hello and welcome you both to Featherston.'

'Thank you.'

She knew that she sounded stiff and stilted, but not even for Rupert's sake could she do anything about it. Adam overwhelmed her with his large presence and enigmatic eyes. He seemed to fill the little hall. Was he really welcoming them *both* to Featherston, or did he really mean his welcome for Rupert only?

The question persisted over the rest of the afternoon as they had tea with Matron, and later as they drove back to London, and in the days that followed.

She couldn't shake it off. Nothing in Adam's manner gave her a clue to his thoughts. To her he had been pleasant and polite, to Rupert very warm and friendly, radiating male charm and strength and, consciously or not, inviting the confidences of the small boy.

He hadn't stayed long in the bungalow, and for the few minutes that he had been there he had chatted mostly to Rupert, an excited, bubbling, uninhibited Rupert full of what he was going to do when they moved in the following week and chattering happily about the new bike Daisy had promised him.

And Adam had encouraged him to talk. It was quite obvious that he was drawn to Rupert, and Rupert to him. It was incredible, almost as though they had known each other for years. Because of their link through Matthew, she wondered, conscious or unconscious? Or was it the charisma that surrounded Adam that drew Rupert to him? She'd watched Adam charm her son with mixed feelings. She'd been part pleased, part fearful, part angry, part jealous even, that he could, in so short a time, exercise an influence over the boy.

She had been relieved when, with a cool goodbye to her, and a light punch on the shoulder and a cheerful, 'See you soon, old chap,' to Rupert, he had left, though the bungalow had seemed strangely empty without him.

Very matey, she had thought sourly, and then, feeling guilty at the sight of Rupert's flushed and happy face, had tried to squash the thought.

And her mixed feelings were still with her when, at the end of the following week, she and Rupert, with the removal van behind them, drove along the cliff road to Featherston.

It was a blustery March day, with the wind driving banks of fluffy white clouds across a pale blue sky which spread like a canopy over the soft green contours of the downs. The wild sea swelled and glittered in the sunlight and crashed noisily against the cliffside, sending plumes of spray high in the air.

Rupert chatted happily all the way, but Daisy found herself answering in monosyllables as they drew nearer their destination. With all her heart she wished that she could feel as he felt about their future, but her reservations about Adam and his attitude towards her made that impossible.

Did he still dislike and distrust her as strongly as ever now that he had met Rupert? Or had he privately acknowledged that she was at least a good mother, however she had measured up as a wife to his best friend, and did he perhaps like her a little better because of it? Would he go out of his way to befriend her son as he had intimated? And if he did, should she encourage him? Supposing that the job at the clinic didn't work out and she and Rupert had to leave in a few months' time, would it be fair to Rupert to have to come to terms with another parting? He seemed at last to have stopped grieving for Aunt Mary, and was now able to talk about her quite cheerfully, but how would he react to the trauma of another broken relationship, should it occur?

Her mind full of unanswered questions, she turned into the lane leading off the cliff road, and a few minutes later into the drive of Featherston Hall. In spite of her reservations, a trickle of excitement coursed through her as they passed the lodges and approached the shining white clinic, full of patients to be nursed and cared for, standing high on the hill. *If* everything turned out all right, this was to be their home, hers and Rupert's, for several, if not many years. Her job should be a safe and secure one with growing responsibilities as the clinic further expanded. *If* she could happily work alongside Adam Torrence. Well, she would damn well do that very thing, she decided grimly, if that was going to be right for Rupert.

She glanced sideways at her son, who was bouncing around with excitement. 'Nearly there,' she told him with a smile. 'Home, sweet home for the foreseeable future.'

Rupert turned a suddenly grave face towards her. 'For always, Mum,' he said seriously. 'Let's stay here forever and ever.' He was very much the little boy seeking reassurance, longing for the stability that he had lost when Aunt Mary died, not the self-assured child that he sometimes appeared to be.

Picking her words carefully, wanting to reassure him, but at the same time not wanting to make any rash promises, Daisy said quietly and firmly, 'Well, love, as you know, I'm on trial for three months before my contract is confirmed; we mustn't forget that.' She smiled confidently at him, pushing aside any doubt she might have about working with Adam. 'But Matron and I get on famously together, and I honestly believe that Featherston will be our home for as long as we want.'

'That's brilliant,' said Rupert as they drew up outside the bungalow. 'Absolutely brilliant.'

CHAPTER FIVE

To DAISY's relief and surprise, considering the trauma of the move from her late aunt's home, it took her and Rupert only a few days to slip into a routine of work, school and play at Featherston.

From day one Rupert settled in at the village school and, in spite of her misgivings about Adam, who appeared quite unruffled by her presence and whom she saw daily, Daisy relished her job at the clinic.

But, however much she enjoyed her work and immersed herself in it, she was always conscious of Adam being around somewhere in the building. To her surprise and annoyance she couldn't seem to get him out of her mind. He was always there, a shadowy presence. And when they met in Matron Browning's office to iron out their plans for the day her heart beat a ridiculous tattoo of pleasure, and she had to steel herself to wish him a cool but friendly, 'Good morning.'

It was ludicrous, she thought, that a man whose motives she half feared should exercise such a hold over her with his charisma. It was, of course, all the more galling because Adam seemed almost indifferent to her. She wasn't even sure if he cared enough to despise her any more for what he thought she had done to Matthew. In fact, he showed no emotion at all when they met. He was always politely distant, handsome and remote, his widow's peak of hair making him look vaguely satanic.

'Get thee behind me, Satan', she commanded silently. And leave me well alone to get on with my life.

And she did. She revelled in the responsibility that her position as assistant matron gave her, but when, a week later, she found herself deputising for Sister McClure on the medical wing, she enjoyed the hands-on nursing quite as much.

And it was in the capacity of relief sister of the medical wing that Daisy assisted Adam one morning as he examined a new admission, a Mrs Jane Taylor—a tired-looking, rather overweight lady of forty-two.

Daisy, squashing the wave of pleasure that washed over her at Adam's proximity, watched with professional approval as he worked skilfully and with unhurried calm. He quickly put the patient at ease, constantly reassuring her as his long, sensitive fingers probed gently, percussing the chest, exploring the abdomen, testing reflexes. He asked many searching questions, and carefully listened to what she had to say in reply, not hurrying her or making her feel inadequate. On account of his thoroughness, it was some time before he completed his top-to-toe examination and straightened up from the bed.

With a smile for Mrs Taylor, he moved across to the window and stared out, obviously deep in thought, giving Daisy the opportunity to smooth sheets and pillows and endeavour to make the rather pathetic-looking lady in the bed comfortable.

After a few moments Adam returned to the bedside. His eyes, dark and expressionless, met Daisy's over the patient. 'May I have the notes again, please, Sister?' he requested, holding out his hand.

Daisy handed him one of the folders from the lower shelf of the examination trolley.

Adam sat on a chair at the side of the bed and, with a murmured, 'Excuse me,' to Mrs Taylor, drew out a thick wodge of papers and began to read.

Daisy finished tidying the instruments on the trolley, and turned back to her patient, who was lying against the pillows, looking pale, agitated and exhausted. 'Are you sure I can't persuade you to have a drink, orange juice or something, or perhaps just a sip of water?' she suggested.

'No, thank you, Sister, not at the moment; I feel I might choke. I have such difficulty in swallowing, and it's sometimes so bad that I throw up.'

Adam looked up from the notes he was studying. 'Well, I hope that we'll be able to help you with that, Mrs Taylor,' he said gently. 'We know that your nausea and vomiting isn't caused by your gall bladder, because you had that removed last year. And on examination then you didn't appear to have a gastric ulcer, though you might have produced one since, so we'll have to eliminate that possibility. Your hiatus hernia might be part of the difficulty, but I believe that the narrowing of your oesophagus, due to a thicking of the walls, is what's making it difficult for you to swallow.

'Tomorrow I'll investigate this further by looking down your throat with an endoscope—that's a fine tube enabling me to examine your gullet and stomach. If I find the oesophagus is narrowed, as I suspect, I will arrange for you to have it stretched by one of our surgeons. This is a minor operation that can be done in our day unit. You'll be there for a few hours, and then return here to your own room.'

'But will I be able to eat and drink again normally, Doctor, if I have this stretch done? I'm fed up with not being able to go out for a meal. This wretched problem is playing havoc with my social life.' She smiled weakly, her pale blue eyes, in a pale, flabby face, looking huge. 'Not that I'm feeling like doing anything much these days. I'm so cold, not just my hands and feet, which have always been a problem, but all over, all through, and I seem to ache in all my joints, and I can't walk far. I'm exhausted half the time, and yet I don't sleep well.'

Her eyes filled with tears. 'It must be hell for my husband and the children, but they've been marvellous. I feel a right old neurotic, and such a trouble to them.'

Adam took one of her hands in his and gave her a smile which lit up his face. 'Well, you're certainly not neurotic, and it's been hell for you too,' he said quietly. 'And your family love you, so of course they're supportive, and quite right too. Now stop worrying about them and think about yourself and getting better. We'll do all that we can to sort out your problems. For starters, I'm going to arrange with Sister for you to have some injections to help control the vomiting, and that will make you feel better almost at once.'

'Thank you, Doctor, that'll be a relief. It's exhausting being sick all the time, and I do feel so tired.' She closed her eyes and lay back against the pillows.

Adam turned to Daisy. 'I think Maxolon ten milligrams, TDS, and a gradual increase in fluid intake should do the trick for the moment, don't you?'

'Yes,' agreed Daisy, 'that should certainly help, but if Mrs Taylor still can't keep anything down, what then?'

'Then we'll have to think about intravenous fluids, but I don't think that's necessary yet; she isn't badly dehydrated, in spite of the sickness, so she must have been retaining something, and I want to keep her swallowing reflexes working as far as possible. And I'm sure that if anyone can you will manage to push the fluids.'

'I'll do my best.'

'I know you will.' He glanced at the dozing patient, then across at Daisy, and murmured softly, 'But then, in spite of everything, you are, and always were, a super nurse.' His eyes met hers and, briefly, she thought she saw warmth and admiration in his, and her breathing quickened. Then the shutters came down, his eyes blanked out, and he became once more his usual inscrutable self, leaving Daisy wondering if she had imagined the change of expression as he had paid her his rather back-handed compliment. He looked down again at his patient and, with a light, reassuring squeeze, released her hand and stood up as she opened her eyes.

'I'll be off now, Mrs Taylor, but I'll see you tomorrow when I do the endoscopy. Now Sister and I are going to have a little chat about some tests that I want you to have over the next few days. Meanwhile, rest and drink as much as possible; that's the best thing you can do at the moment. Isn't that right, Sister?' he said quietly, turning to Daisy for confirmation.

Fleetingly their eyes met again, and again, annoyingly, Daisy felt her heartbeat quicken. This was ridiculous. She nodded and said steadily, 'Indeed it is, Doctor.' She smiled down at the patient. 'I'll send a nurse in to give you your first injection shortly, Mrs Taylor. Take little sips of water when you can; even in minute amounts it'll help and I'm sure that eventually you'll get some to stay down and then we can try something more interesting and nourishing than water.'

Adam looked thoughtful as he stood back to let her pass through the doorway, and then waited while she gave instructions to a passing staff nurse about Mrs Taylor's injection. They walked in silence side by side down the long corridor towards her office. Daisy was very conscious of his large, lean presence beside her, and when, after a few moments, he asked, glancing sideways at her, 'Any ideas about our new patient?' she found herself replying breathlessly and rather brusquely, as they entered the office.

'Not many.'

This just wouldn't do. If only she weren't so conscious of him!

She sat down behind her desk and made a great effort to compose herself, squash her errant reactions and think about the patient, as Adam, crossing one long, neatly trousered leg over the other, took the chair opposite. In a commendably normal voice she said, 'She's clearly generally not well and is suffering from an oesophageal reflux and, by the way she described her hands and feet as often cold and alternately white, blue and bright pink, I suspect that she is suffering from Raynaud's phenomenon. Obviously her circulation's extremely poor—her fingers are thickened and scaly as if they've been ulcerated. But that doesn't explain her other symptoms—lethargy, pain in joints and so on—does it?'

'No, because Raynaud's, in this case, is probably the symptom of something else. Do you know anything about scleroderma or systemic sclerosis, as it is sometimes called?'

'I've heard of it, but I've never come across it, and there's not much in the textbooks about it.'

'No, it's a very rare condition that can attack many vital organs, though it usually progresses slowly. Only a handful of people in a million acquire this disease, and I rather fear that our Mrs Taylor might be one of them. Of course, I want to do more tests—a skin biopsy and so on—and I shall refer her to an expert for an opinion; but from what she had already told us, and from what I gleaned from her GP's letter and other consultants' notes, I don't think there's much doubt as to the diagnosis.'

'Poor Mrs Taylor,' Daisy said with compassion, concentrating on what Adam was saying, her mind and thoughts firmly fixed on her patient. 'What can you do for her?'

Adam shrugged eloquently. 'Not a lot, I'm afraid. Offer palliative treatment, like the stretch for the oesophagus and medication to make swallowing easier; there's some good stuff on the market now. And, of course, give her analgesics for the joint pains. But scleroderma is an auto-immune disorder, attacking the body's own immune system, and there is no cure at present. I understand, though, that there's a trial currently being conducted using photophoresis and a drug called Methoxsalen.'

'Really?' Daisy brightened. 'So there's some hope, then.'

'Well, as I say, it's only just underway; it'll be ages before the results are known and any firm conclusions drawn, let alone treatments formulated. All I know is that the trial treatment involves removing blood from the patient, introducing Methoxsalen and subjecting it to ultraviolet light, which results in alteration of the immune cells, before returning the blood to the body.'

'Well, even if it doesn't lead to a cure, perhaps the information gleaned will be useful in understanding the disease better. Do you think people are able to live anything like normal lives with this wretched affliction?'

'From what I have heard, people do in varying degrees, according to age and the advancement of the condition. It's incredible how some of them carry on, though I must point out that my information comes second hand, through what I've read or discussed with the handful of colleagues who know something about it. This is my first head-on experience. The trouble is, sufferers are usually debilitated by the multiplicity of symptoms—they often find the least exercise exhausting. It's frustrating and depressing, but unless one of the vital organs is clearly affected they seem to cope.'

'So we should be able to get Mrs Taylor back on her feet.'

'Certainly. She'll begin to feel better for a while anyway, once we've got her swallowing properly and she can keep some food down, and we can also give her something to improve her circulation, which will be a great help. And if, as I suspect, she has an underactive thyroid and a low metabolic rate, causing her to put on weight, and lose some hair, we can of course do something about that.

'When she goes home we'll give her a list of medication for her doctor to prescribe, and alert him to the seriousness of her condition. He sounds like a good man, but, because so little is known about scleroderma, like most GPs, he's working in the dark, and perhaps underestimates the problem.'

'Surely there's some literature available about it?'

'I believe there's an organisation, the Raynaud's and Scleroderma Association, which seems very active with information and has been involved with this trial, but how much your busy GP knows about the disease is difficult to say; very little, I should imagine. Meanwhile, we do our best for our patient, and together help her to come to terms with her condition, yes?'

'Of course.'

Adam raised his eyebrows and gave her a smile, a warm, easy, friendly smile, and she found herself smiling just as easily in return as he added, 'And talking of busy GPs and doctors in general, I'm due at the day unit to do some insurance examinations, so I'll be back to do the rest of my round this afternoon, if that's all right with you, Daisy?'

'Yes, quite all right, Adam.'

In spite of their use of Christian names, it was an almost formal, purely professional exchange, and yet Daisy felt that there was something special about it. Briefly, without a word being said, the barriers that Adam had erected between them on account of Matthew dissolved as they sat there smiling at each other across the desk. It was a companionable moment, without any overtones on either side, and Daisy was conscious that for once they were both quite at ease with each other.

After a long second Adam, still smiling, nodded. 'Good,' he said, 'then I'll be off.' Unfolding his long legs, he stood up and, with a few easy strides, crossed the room. He paused at the door and turned. 'By the way, I should have asked before, only we always seem to be so damned busy when we meet; how are you and Rupert settling in?'

His eyes, still gleaming with a smiling warmth, crinkling at the corners, met hers across the small space between her desk and the door. But in that moment, as his eyes claimed hers, they changed, darkened, and the smile went out of them, to be replaced by. . .by what? A look that was fathoms-deep, that seemed to be drawing her to him. His eyes were full of. . . No, Adam didn't even like her. A hushed, breathless silence descended on the room.

Daisy felt her blood pumping madly in her chest and drumming loudly in her ears as for an endless moment they stared at each other across the silent room. She wanted the moment to go on forever.

As if from a distance she heard herself say faintly, replying to the question that he had asked aeons ago, 'Fine, Adam, thank you; we're just fine. Rupert loves his school, and has already made some friends, and we have delightful neighbours—the Hills.' The banal words came out automatically, through lips that hardly moved. It was a weird but wonderful sensation that went on and on, divorced from real time, as she almost drowned in the depths of his eyes. And for one incredible moment she wondered if she was going to faint.

She was conscious that Adam was speaking, his deep, rich voice seeming to come from a distance too. 'Oh, yes, the Hills—Steven, the senior radiographer, and his family.' His eyes remained locked on to hers. They were talking about the Hills, but their eyes were saying something else. This was madness, nonsense.

She felt that she was existing on two levels of awareness, floating on air and at the same time struggling to hang on to normality. She said breathlessly, 'That's right; Janice, his wife, is a lovely person, and their three children are super. Rupert and Tom, who is nine, seem to be getting on famously, and Rupert, being an only child, is intrigued by the twins, Alice and Elizabeth, though they are only six.' The words poured out easily, though her mind was only half on what she was saying. It was like seeing oneself in a dream.

'And you, Daisy?' Adam asked in a drawling, soft, far-away voice. 'Are you getting on famously?'

She wanted to lower her eyes, escape his gaze, but couldn't. 'Oh, yes, I'm loving my work,' she breathed.

'And your leisure time?'

She said with a stiff little smile, 'I haven't much of that by the time I get home and see to things like ironing and so on and helping Rupert with his homework.'

'You should join the social club and get out a bit—you know what they say about all work and no play. . .'

His voice trailed off, but his dark, gleaming eyes held hers for a moment longer, until at last she pulled hers away from his, looking down at her desk and fiddling with some papers. She breathed in deeply; she had broken the spell, real or imagined. Had these last few hypnotic moments really happened? And if they had, had they meant anything to Adam? She glanced swiftly at him, taking care not to meet his eyes. He looked the picture of normality, as solid and calm and handsome as ever in a dark grey suit, snowy white shirt and a soberly striped tie.

A small sigh escaped her. Everything *looked* normal, *was* normal, she told herself. With an effort she dragged up a quirky smile and said brightly, 'Social clubs, leisure time—there speaks the lucky, fancy-free bachelor.'

She expected Adam to laugh and make some clever, sophisticated remark, but he didn't. 'Lucky?' he said thoughtfully. 'I'm not sure about that. It's lonely sometimes being a bachelor, whether or not fancy-free.'

For someone so large and competent and in control he looked suddenly young and vulnerable, more like the man she had known years ago. Daisy's heart lurched and a wave of sympathy washed over her as she remembered his partner in Africa. He must miss her dreadfully, even if she hadn't been the great love of his life.

She stood up, moved round the desk and walked towards him, holding out her hands, feeling all at once confident; their roles reversed, she wanted to touch him, comfort him. He made no attempt to take her hands, so she reached up and put them on his shoulders. 'Adam,' she said softly, 'don't be sad; you'll meet somebody one day whom you will want to marry, and you'll have a family. You won't remain a lonely bachelor forever.'

He gave a little snort of hard laughter, and his mouth twisted sardonically at the corners. He stared down at her disbelievingly, and said in a harsh, bitter voice, 'You've got to be kidding, Daisy. You should know. What the hell does falling in love have to do with it, unless that love is returned? I made the mistake of falling in love once, but never again. She had eyes only for someone else, and like a fool I backed off, leaving the field free for him—and a fat lot of good that did anyone.'

'I'm so sorry, Adam; you must have loved her very much to make such a sacrifice for her. Did she have any idea how you felt?'

Adam gave her a long, penetrating, almost puzzled look, then shook his head and said slowly, in a low voice, 'No, Daisy, I don't think she did; as I said, she only had eyes for the other chap; I don't think anyone else existed for her then. Of course later. . .'

His voice trailed away and he frowned, and, as if suddenly becoming conscious of her hands on his shoulders, he lifted them off. Still holding them, he then took a small step backwards. He squeezed her fingers, none too gently, before letting them go.

'But enough of this introspection,' he said briskly. 'I must go now; I've work to do and so have you. I'll see you this afternoon. Goodbye.'

He didn't wait for her reply, but turned smartly and let himself out of the door, closing it quietly behind him.

Daisy stared blankly at the closed door as she heard his footsteps receding down the corridor. She felt a strange mixture of emotions as she thought about what had just taken place between them.

There had been the long eye contact when he had seemed to bend her to his will, seemed to be telling her something—so ephemeral in retrospect that she wondered if it had been all in her imagination. But the tail-end of her conversation with him had not been imaginary. For once, for a few minutes, when he had admitted to having been in love, he had forgotten to blame her for what she had done to Matthew and had treated her like an old friend in whom he could confide. Whatever else had happened this morning that was a huge step forward in their relationship, if only it would last.

Poor Adam. What a sad love life he had had, in spite of his good looks and his masculinity and charisma, which had always attracted women by the dozen. How strange that he could have had the pick of the female staff in those early days at St Vincent's, and yet had fallen for someone who had not returned his love. And then he had found consolation with Kate in Africa, but she had died, and instead of becoming bitter, as he might well have done, he had matured into a fine, sensitive man and a dedicated doctor. He was wonderful to work with, and perhaps after today's 'confession' he would be more friendly on the personal front.

With a sigh, she returned to her desk and gazed unseeingly at the papers strewn on it, then methodically began to sort them into some sort of order and return them to the correct folders. She worked automatically, her thoughts still with Adam and what he had revealed about being lonely. Her mind drifted back to the past when she, Matthew and Adam had all been at the beginning of their careers, boisterous, full of energy, full of hope for the future. They were all going to conquer the world of medicine, and they had worked hard and played hard.

Played hard! Who had Adam been dating when she and Matthew were already 'an item'? She could only remember Paula Jones or Brenda Marshall as anything like steady companions. Which of the two had turned him down and so devastated him? They'd both married other young doctors, but which of them had jilted Adam? She had no idea.

Resolutely she dismissed her thoughts as a knock came at the door. 'Come in,' she called, and Joy Kent, the staff nurse whom she had delegated to give Mrs Taylor her injection, bounced into the room.

'I've given Mrs Taylor her Maxolon,' she reported, 'and recorded it, and tried to persuade her to have a drink, but she was most reluctant. Do we know what's wrong with her yet? I know she has difficulty swallowing and is nauseous, and she's tired but doesn't sleep well, but why? Does our gorgeous and extremely clever medical officer know?'

'Well, he's got to do more tests before confirming, but he believes that she's suffering from scleroderma, or systemic sclerosis, accompanied by Raynaud's phenomenon. Ever heard of scleroderma?'

'Indeed I have, though it's pretty rare. There was a case in my last hospital—a lovely old lady who'd had the condition for years, and also had Raynaud's. Her circulation was so bad that she'd had both feet and one hand amputated. She had swallowing difficulties too, and she was in for investigations into her liver, yet somehow she remained cheerful.'

'Poor old love. Let's hope and pray our patient won't ever get that bad. By the way, Joy, you'd best keep this info about your previous patient to yourself; we don't want it inadvertently leaking out to Mrs Taylor and frightening her to death.'

'You've got to be kidding,' Joy said fiercely, looking at Daisy in astonishment as an angry stain flushed her usually pale cheeks. She tucked a strand of red hair back under her cap. Her green eyes flashed. 'You don't really think that I'd do anything so cruel and irresponsible as to pass this sort of bad news on to a patient, do you? Because if you do, then I might as well take off here and now.'

Daisy, seeing how angry Joy was, realised that for the first time she'd got a small, but fiery, staff crisis on her hands which she had to deal with immediately. She looked at her colleague in genuine surprise, and sought to placate her.

'Of course I don't think that you would divulge anything to a patient,' she said calmly. 'The thought hadn't even crossed my mind. But everyone may not be as professionally discreet as you. Younger nurses, without the experience that you and I have, domestics, patients even, may overhear something and gossip. Which is why I think we should keep this little story to ourselves. Amputations are always dramatic and there's always somebody ready to sensationalise such incidents and make deliberate or accidental capital out of it, as I'm sure you'll agree.'

'Well, yes, I suppose that's true,' said Joy reluctantly, somewhat mollified by Daisy's words. She straightened her cap on her thick, wiry curls. 'Just as long as you don't think that I'm capable of any such thing.'

'No question of that,' Daisy said firmly. 'In fact I would like you to special Mrs Taylor when you're on duty, and choose someone to take over when you're not. Prepare a fluid balance chart, and press fluids, and solids, too, of course, when you can persuade the patient to try to eat. She's having an oesophageal stretch tomorrow, so might feel more like eating within the next few days. Jane Taylor is *your* patient, Joy; you take responsibility for her; she's all yours.'

Joy beamed across the desk at Daisy. 'You mean that?' she asked. 'You're not just saying that because I lost my rag?'

'Not at all; I wouldn't put my patients in such jeopardy.' They smiled at each other, and Daisy gave an inward sigh of relief, knowing that she had won that round and retained her authority.

Adam returned to finish his round at two-thirty, his manner rather austere and professional. His morning visit, with all its peculiar undercurrents, might never have happened.

His voice was cold and formal as he said, 'Good afternoon, Sister; who do you want me to see first?'

Daisy's heart sank. She hadn't known what to expect, but it certainly wasn't this deliberate coldness, which seemed to freeze her out. He was obviously already regretting any earlier intimacies so was pretending that they had never happened. He was warning her off, challenging her not to become too personal. Well, if that was what he wanted, he could have it. She would be totally professional.

She said quietly, 'Mr Lyons, please, Doctor, room five. He's pressing to go home, though the ulcers on his heels and sacral area are still needing attention. Quite honestly, I think he's afraid of becoming too dependent on care, knowing that it can't go on forever.'

At once Adam's stern features relaxed and softened. 'Poor old chap, I suppose he'll go back to the old routine of living on his own, sitting all day and half the night in a chair, suffering from near malnutrition and, because of his poor condition, getting pressures sores.'

'Yes, I'm afraid that's the general picture. I hope you can talk him into staying a bit longer. Given another week we should be able to get those ulcers healed, and he would at least go home in good nick.'

'Ideally he should come in permanently to our long-stay nursing-home unit.'

'I've already thought about that, and tentatively broached the subject; he was mildly interested. But I didn't like to press it because it suddenly occurred to me that he wouldn't be able to afford the fees, even if he was willing to come. His insurance, which takes care of acute nursing fees, wouldn't cover long-term care and he only has a one-bedroomed flat to sell, so the money from that wouldn't last him long. If he goes anywhere it will have to be to a council rest home.'

Adam looked thoughtful. 'Perhaps the local authority would help him come here to the clinic. Let's get in touch with social services and make a few enquiries and then tackle our Mr Lyons again. Meanwhile, we'll try to persuade him to stay for another week or so. I think with our combined powers we ought to be able to do that, don't you?' he said, giving her a wide smile, inviting her confirmation that they would work together as a team.

'Oh, yes, I'm sure we can,' she replied firmly, smiling back at him. Her heart lifted; his coldness had gone. One couldn't fault him as a doctor. It was as if, having established the fact that he wanted no personal intimacy with her, he was making it clear that he was happy to work with her for his patients' sake, and knew that she felt the same. It was going to be all right; at least on the professional front they would always work together amicably. And that was all that really mattered. As for what might happen on the personal front, that, she felt, was in the lap of the gods.

'Good,' said Adam cheerfully. 'Then let's go and beard this stubborn old Lyons in his den, and see if we can knock some sense into him!'

CHAPTER SIX

AND they had succeeded, Daisy reflected as hours later she lay in bed trying to get to sleep, while reviewing the ups and downs of the day.

How kind Adam had been with Mr Lyons as he had gently bullied the old gentleman into agreeing to stay at Featherston for another fortnight.

And the rest of the afternoon round had gone smoothly too, revealing no surprises such as the morning had yielded. No strange diagnoses, no unusual conditions had come to light; everything had been quite normal—at least, as normal as any hospital ever could be.

With Mrs Long in room ten, a tense, nervous, excitable lady, Adam had been endlessly patient and reassuring, carefully explaining to her that she needed further tests to confirm whether or not she was suffering from hyperparathyroidism.

'Don't be alarmed by the long name,' he'd told her gently. 'It simply means the small pea-shaped parathyroid glands, which are embedded in the thyroid gland in your neck, are overactive.'

He had even drawn her a little diagram illustrating the position of the thyroid gland so that she could clearly see what he was talking about.

'And if it is confirmed that you have a problem with these glands,' he'd continued, 'you can have surgery to remove any excess parathyroid tissue. It's an operation that has been performed frequently with great success, and I promise you you will feel a different person once it has been done. It will give you a new lease of life. Isn't that true, Sister?' he'd asked, looking across at Daisy who'd been standing at the other side of the bed.

It had been a conspiratorial, compelling look, she now recalled, asking her to agree with him whole-heartedly in order to reassure the anxious lady. And she had understood, marvelling again at Adam's patience and understanding, and had smiled at him and the patient, whose hand she had given a squeeze. 'What Dr Torrence has said is perfectly true, Mrs Long,' she'd said firmly. 'I've nursed many patients with your condition and they've all done well following their operation.'

Adam's detailed explanation and patience had paid dividends, for Mrs Long had been much reassured. 'Isn't Dr Torrence lovely? Such a good doctor, and so handsome,' she had enthused when later Daisy had called in to say goodnight before going off duty. 'And those dark, romantic eyes. . .' She'd rolled her own. 'Just seeing him is enough to make you feel better.' And, poorly as she was, she had actually laughed.

Similar sentiments had been expressed by many of the other patients Adam had seen that afternoon. Even the male patients were impressed by him, and they weren't influenced by his good looks, but entirely by his reassuring manner and expertise.

His good looks! Well, he had those in abundance, but then he always had had—and a strong, sometimes overexuberant personality to match. But maturity suited him; it had enhanced his youthful good looks, calmed and broadened his personality, lent him the authority that as a younger man, like Matthew, he had not possessed. Would Matthew, too, have improved with time, had he lived?

Daisy stared into the darkness, seeing both men, but most of all seeing Adam's eyes, those dark, long-lashed, enigmatic eyes that Mrs Long had drooled over, deep-set in that lean, handsome face. Eyes which had almost mesmerised her this morning.

Her heartbeat quickened at the memory. Had he done that deliberately, or had she only imagined the way his eyes had bored into hers, bewitching her with a kind of magic?

She gave a great sigh. So Adam Torrence was a brilliant, charismatic doctor, and the clinic was lucky to have his devoted services, and she was lucky to be working with him. Well, she would make the most of it. She had to make the most of it for Rupert's sake. But if only Adam. . .she thought wistfully. If only Adam what? 'Liked and respected me a little more as a person, as well as a nurse,' she whispered to herself. 'It would make everything perfect here at Featherston.'

Well, perhaps one day he would, she mused. He had in general been a little more friendly today, quite apart from the intimate disclosures of the morning and the heart-stopping eye-to-eye contact. He had been less remote as they'd discussed their patients over tea in her office and as he'd prepared to leave, following the afternoon round, he'd turned at the door and said with quiet sincerity, 'Thanks for all your help and support, Daisy. We've had our difficulties of one kind or another today, but we sorted them out together. We make a good team, do we not?'

He'd smiled gently, and her foolish heart had flipped at that and the small compliment, though he'd meant it only on a professional level.

'Oh, yes, we do,' she had replied a trifle breathlessly.

Remembering now, as she waited for sleep to come,

she thought how ridiculous it was that a woman of her age and experience should be so easily rattled by a smile and a few kind words, especially from a man who, on a personal level, didn't even like or approve of her.

It was on this thought that eventually she drifted into unconsciousness and confused dreams involving Adam and Matthew. Surprisingly, because they had been such great friends, they were fighting as if they hated each other, sort of shadow-boxing angrily. Rupert was there too, standing between the two men, looking small and vulnerable, and she was trying to snatch him away.

She woke in the morning with a headache, a hazy recollection of her unpleasant dreams, and a determination to put Adam Torrence out of her mind. She knew that she mustn't allow him to dominate her thoughts as he had been lately, and she mustn't read anything into the softening of his attitude at work the day before, or the seeming intensity of that long, lingering look. Surely it had meant little or nothing to him, if indeed it had really happened. She would try to forget it.

Because over the next few weeks she was rushed off her feet covering for Sister McClure, this determination not to think about Adam on a personal basis should have been easy but, to her dismay, she discovered that it wasn't. Only long practice enabled her to squash thoughts of Adam and all personal matters while she attended to patients. But, against her will, she found herself looking forward to his frequent visits to the wing, and on each occasion experienced a little frisson of pleasure when he appeared. And when he wasn't there in the flesh, in rare quiet moments he continued to haunt her thoughts.

Off duty, she kept herself busy with household chores, and tending the hitherto neglected garden which was now full of signs of spring, with daffodils and forsythia in full bloom. But even at home she found that being busy physically was not enough to keep her mind from straying to Adam. She was always aware that he wasn't far away, in the lodge, or in the clinic itself, and she found herself wishing that he might suddenly appear on her doorstep, as he had once before.

Occasionally she wondered if he ever gave a passing thought to her or Rupert when he was off duty. He had spoken once of getting to know Rupert better, but had so far made no attempt to do so. Had he forgotten that he had made the suggestion or simply changed his mind?

As for Rupert, it was ironic that just when she needed him most he, who normally would have taken up much of her time and attention and put everything else out of her mind, was these days seldom in the house for long. When he wasn't at school he spent most of his time with his friends, the Hills, or happily playing with the other children on the little staff estate until dusk. It was the perfect set-up for a fatherless only child, and he already seemed to have been absorbed into the little community.

It was almost perfect for a single parent too, Daisy discovered as the days passed. She had an endless stream of invitations to coffee or drinks, and offers to care for Rupert when she was on duty, from her neighbours. Life had definitely taken an upward turn in the weeks that she and Rupert had been at Featherston.

Only Adam remained a problem for her to come to terms with. For, although she continued to try hard to treat him as just another colleague and dismiss any other feelings she might have for him, her resolve was shattered by a deep-seated longing to put things right between them. More than anything she wanted him to accept her version of events relating to the break-up of her marriage. She desperately wanted him not to blame her for what had happened, and knew that she would not be truly happy until she had convinced him. Nothing less would do.

In fact, winning his regard had become increasingly important to her, almost an obsession. Was it an impossible dream to establish her innocence with the mature, authoritative Adam, the self-assured man, the good doctor? Surely the memory of Matthew wouldn't always come between them, stop them being at the very least good friends? Surely Adam wouldn't always despise her?

It was a chilling thought, for the more she saw of the calm, kindly man at work, the more she wanted to establish a truly friendly, or perhaps even closer, relationship with him, she realised with a shock. For, try as she might, she couldn't entirely dismiss the deep emotional and sensual feelings she began having about him. The very sight or sound of him stirred her senses.

In theory there were plenty of opportunities for her to pursue her dream of friendship, for he was on the medical wing most days, examining difficult cases and new admissions, and they had many chances to talk. But the right moment never seemed to present itself. As always, Adam was pleasant, courteous and cheerful to patients and staff alike, but because she wanted something special from him she almost resented the fact that he treated her in the same pleasant but purely professional manner as he did everyone else.

This was regularly illustrated when, after doing a round, they would return to the office to discuss patients and treatments over their coffee or tea, and although Daisy always hoped that he might alter his attitude when they were alone together he never did. There was no repeat of the intimate moments they had shared briefly on that one day when he had disclosed the facts about Kate, his partner in Africa, and had talked about his other true love whom he had left behind in England. He had seemed so vulnerable then, so reachable.

But since that day he had shown no inclination to talk, and certainly not to confide. As soon as they had finished their business he normally left the office with a polite but cool farewell, leaving her feeling deflated, helpless and resigned, and sometimes angry.

It was therefore a complete surprise when one afternoon he remained seated and made no attempt to leave after he had finished writing up the last medication.

After a moment, Daisy asked rather hesitantly, 'Would you—like another cup of tea?'

'Please.' He pushed his cup and saucer across the desk and watched as she filled it. 'Thank you,' he said with the slightest of smiles as she pushed it back towards him.

Daisy inclined her head. 'A pleasure,' she murmured inanely, her heart beating fast as she looked at his inscrutable, handsome face. What did he want, why was he staying today, why didn't he just go as usual? 'Is there something else? Have I forgotten anything, done something dreadful? Are you going to give me a right telling-off?' she asked lightly, to break the awkward moment.

Adam shook his head and gave her a quirky half-smile. 'No, as always the round went off most efficiently; nothing was overlooked or forgotten.'

'Oh, good,' she said lamely, looking down at her desk and shuffling some papers around.

He reached across and covered her fluttering hands with his own. She found his touch unnerving. Her heart bumped uncomfortably. With iron control she stopped herself from trembling. 'Daisy,' he said quietly, 'stop agitating.'

'I'm not agitating,' she said sharply, pulling her hands from beneath his. 'I'm just wondering what's keeping you here today; you usually can't wait to disappear directly we've finished discussing treatments and so on.'

Adam raised an eyebrow, sat back in his chair, and looked at her thoughtfully. 'And does that bother you?'

She shook her head. 'No, of course not.'

'Good.' He gave her a wry smile. 'Well, don't be alarmed at my change of tactics; I only want to talk to Rupert.'

'Rupert!' She stared at him in astonishment; whatever could he mean? What on earth could he have to say about Rupert?

'Naturally I'm interested in the boy's welfare; you must know that,' he said mildly.

'Because he's Matthew's son?'

'Of course.' He leaned forward, smiling faintly. 'You shouldn't be so surprised, Daisy. If you remember, I said that I hoped we would get better acquainted. Now he's had time to settle, I'd simply like to know how he's getting on at school and so forth. Is he enjoying his new life?'

She would have liked to say that it was none of his business, that he hadn't bothered all these years to find out how Rupert was doing, so why show an interest now? But she knew that was unfair, for, although she and Adam had parted at daggers drawn when she'd left Matthew, he had written later from Africa when he had learned of Matthew's death, offering sympathy and help, an offer which she had refused. She had made it quite clear then that she wanted nothing to do with him. She said stiffly, 'Rupert's fine; he's a very happy little boy.'

'Good; it must be difficult for you to give him all the time he needs when you work such long hours.'

Daisy felt her face flush as a wave of anger suffused her. 'Are you suggesting that I neglect my son?' she asked coldly, through tight lips.

'Certainly not; the thought hadn't even crossed my mind. I simply meant what I said. It must be difficult for you.'

Her burst of anger subsided; he was obviously being genuinely sincere. 'I'm sorry; I'm a bit spiky about the subject as I always *do* feel that I should give Rupert more time. I feel quite guilty about being on duty so much when he's home from school, but he seems to be having a whale of a time with his new friends, and doesn't appear to miss me at all. In fact,' she said, unaware that she sounded rather wistful, 'you might say that *he's* neglecting *me*, he's becoming so independent.' She gave a tremulous little laugh.

'He would miss you if you weren't there, you know,' said Adam, his voice gentle, his manner suddenly full of warmth and understanding. 'Don't worry, Daisy; he's able to enjoy himself because he knows that you're never far away. He's revelling in his new life because he feels secure.'

'Do you really think so?' she asked in an uncertain voice.

Adam nodded. 'I do,' he said firmly. 'Don't doubt yourself; you're doing a fine job with the boy, without keeping him tied to your apron-strings. He's paying you a compliment by feeling free to go off and play with his friends.'

'Really? I sometimes feel that all he needs from me these days is bed and board. Oh, and of course his bicycle,' she added wryly.

'Oh, yes, the famous bike. He told me about it the day I called at your bungalow before you moved in; he was full of it.'

'We're going to shop for it this coming Saturday. Miraculously, I have the weekend off.'

'Anywhere particular in mind?'

'Any reputable cycle shop in Brighthelm. I've been looking at the advertisements in the paper, and there seem to be all sorts of good deals on at the moment.'

'Try Blackfords in the high street. I often pop in there for car accessories, and they've a great range of bikes and a very helpful staff.'

'Thank you, I'll do that.'

'How are you going to transport the bike home? You won't get it in your dinky little car,' he said, with a smile.

'I'll have it delivered.'

'That's a pity; Rupert will be disappointed that he can't have it straight away. Look, Daisy, let me make a suggestion. I've got to go into Brighthelm on Saturday, so why don't I take you and Rupert with me and bring you and the bike back? There'll be plenty of room in my car for all three of us and the new bike.'

The suggestion took her totally by surprise, and for a moment she could only stare speechlessly at Adam's calm, smiling face. Was this the olive-branch she had been longing for? Was he holding out the hand of friendship? She said in a startled and rather breathy voice, 'Adam, it's very kind of you, but I can't ask you to do that.'

'You're not asking, I'm offering.'

'But why? You don't want to bother with us on your day off.'

'Surely that's for me to decide. Unless you think that Rupert would rather go with you alone. The last thing I want to do is muscle in on the boy's pleasure.'

'Oh, no, it's not that,' she said quickly. 'In fact I think he would be thrilled to have a man around to help him choose his bike. Perhaps the one and only thing he misses here is. . .' Her voice trailed off and her cheeks reddened. She had been going to say 'is a father', but suddenly realised how inappropriate that was to say to Adam Torrence of all people.

But Adam must have guessed what she was going to say, for he suggested softly, 'A father figure, a role model? All of the children round her come from two-parent families, so a bright boy like Rupert is bound to have noticed the difference between his circumstances and theirs, and made comparisons. I know that you must have told him when his father died, and presumably let him believe that you were living *en famille* at the time, but what else did you tell him? Does he know, for instance, that I was his father's best friend?'

'No, he only knows that you were a friend to both of us, and he doesn't know you because you went to Africa when he was a baby. I only ever talked to him in general about the past when he began to ask questions. And you're quite right, Adam, I have let him believe that we were all living together when Matthew died, and I know that I'm right to do so. He's still too young to face the true facts about his father, if he ever needs to know them. I want him to think of Matthew with affection. I see no reason to tell him the truth—that I left his father because he was an aggressive alcoholic; it would be rather pointless.'

'I'll go along with that—it *would* be pointless to besmirch Matthew's memory. I'm sorry you still find it necessary to keep up that pretence, Daisy. You could at least be honest with me after all this time and tell me the truth about what happened when you split up. When I came home on short leave Matthew told me everything, and I can't believe that he lied to me then about your affair with this other chap. Why should he?'

'Because it was easier for him to pretend that there was someone else rather than acknowledge that it was because of his own failings that I had left him; and also to put you off the scent. And he wanted to enlist your sympathy, knowing that the truth would upset you. In fact, he probably half convinced himself it was true by the time he told you. But I'm being honest, Adam, if only you could see it. I didn't *want* to see anything wrong in him, but I *had* to leave him when he started knocking me about. . .*please* don't ask for all the sordid details! Remember, I had Rupert to think of.'

She looked imploringly at him, begging him to believe her. But Adam just stared at her across the desk, his eyes pebble-hard. She lifted her chin defiantly and met them unflinchingly.

After a few moments' silence, he said in a harsh voice, 'I can't believe Matthew ever wanted to hurt you. He loved you too much, and he would never have hurt his son. You should have stayed with him, Daisy.' His tone was accusing, unforgiving.

'Oh, Adam, you didn't see much of him in those last

years; you were away a lot. He'd changed from the fun-loving, irresponsible but kind man you knew into an unreliable, gambling drunk. He gambled everything away, mortgaged the house to the hilt, surrendered insurance policies. That's why I have to work now and can't give Rupert all my time and attention, because I have to earn a living.'

To her horror, her eyes suddenly filled with tears as memories of those last months with Matthew came flooding back. Was Adam right—should she have stayed with him? An all too familiar wave of guilt swamped her. Could she have saved Matthew from an early death if she had stayed with him? Had she used the baby Rupert as an excuse to leave her husband?

Adam's face swam into view, blurred by her tears. He still looked stern and forbidding, but there was a hint now of compassion in his eyes; the unforgiving hardness had gone. He handed her a large, snow-white handkerchief from his breast pocket. 'Here,' he said, 'use this, not one of those paper things.'

'Thank you.' Daisy gave him a watery smile, wiped her eyes and blew her nose. 'I'm sorry about this; I'm not much given to crying. I'll launder your hanky before I return it to you.'

He said impatiently. 'No matter—what's a handkerchief? I'm sorry to have upset you, Daisy, raking up painful memories, but I find it hard to come to terms with what happened between you and Matthew, whatever the truth of it is.'

'I've told you the truth.' Daisy felt drained of emotion; her voice was flat and colourless. 'Why won't you believe me, Adam?' She looked at him across the desk, her violet-blue eyes pleading for his understanding.

He shrugged. 'Because if I believe you it makes Matthew out to have been a liar, and I don't think that he would have lied to me.'

'But you think *I* can,' she said bitterly.

Adam said slowly, almost hesitantly, regarding her in a puzzled fashion, looking for once less than utterly sure of himself, 'No, no, not normally, of course you wouldn't lie, but I think that in this instance you're deceiving yourself as to why you left Matthew, and putting all the blame on him. I can appreciate that things were tough for you, that he did drink too much and your marriage was going through a bad patch, when at that crucial moment you met someone else. Perhaps you weren't so involved as Matthew thought, and only used this other chap to bring him to his senses. Isn't that what really happened, my dear Daisy?' He sounded almost pleading. 'I could understand that. You didn't really mean to leave him for good, did you?'

Daisy breathed in hard and tried to hold down her rising temper. She said in a low, icy voice, staring at him across the desk, 'How dare you patronise me with such a suggestion, Adam Torrence? I left Matthew for the reasons that I have stated, and that's the plain, unvarnished truth. You'd better believe it.'

'You're asking me to believe that what Matthew said was a tissue of lies, a cover-up, or a figment of his imagination!' Adam exclaimed in an incredulous voice.

'Yes.' She continued to stare at him, and he stared back. Her moment of anger began to subside, replaced by a wave of sadness. It was devastating that he, the man she so wanted to impress with the truth, was determined to misread her words and actions to protect Matthew's memory. His loyalty to his dead friend was extraordinary, and seemingly unshakeable.

After a few moments, Adam said gently, 'Daisy, I didn't mean to patronise or hurt you; it's the last thing I want to do. I was just putting forward what I thought was a reasonable explanation for what happened.'

'By insinuating that I might be half telling the truth, at least about Matthew's drinking; by giving me a way out to justify my actions?'

'By rationalising what you did.'

'That happens to fit in with what Matthew told you, and yet shows me as not quite scarlet woman you thought I was,' she said bitterly.

'Something like that,' Adam conceded abruptly, as if suddenly wearying of the whole discussion. 'Look, we seem to have reached an impasse, so let's call a truce over this and agree to differ, for Rupert's sake if nothing else. Don't let's spoil his outing on Saturday.'

Daisy looked at him in amazement. She could hardly believe what she was hearing. Her senses reeled. She said unbelievingly, 'Do you mean that you *still* want to take us to get his bike after all that we've just said to each other?'

'Of course,' he said firmly. 'Nothing's changed where Rupert's concerned, and surely we're adult enough to take this in our stride? We've aired our views about something that happened a long time ago. I'm willing to put it behind us, if you are. I still want to get to know your son better, and the Saturday trip is an ideal opportunity to start, don't you agree?'

She drew in a deep, harsh breath. Did he really mean it? He sounded very sincere. Her mind grappled with what he had said. How could he suggest that they carry on as if nothing had happened? It was incredible. And yet he made it seem so sensible, so civilised, and above all in Rupert's best interest. That was really the central theme of his suggestion. She simply had to accept that though he still considered her guilty of having an affair of some sort, and deserting Matthew, he was ready to suppress his reservations about her for Rupert's sake.

Could she argue with that? No! In her heart she knew that Rupert would benefit from Adam's friendship; they had taken to each other at their first meeting. At this moment in time, Rupert needed a traditional role model; it would give him no end of confidence. And Adam had made it clear that he considered himself the ideal person for the part—and, of course, he was right.

She would have to ask Rupert if he would like Adam to come with them on Saturday, but in her heart she knew that he would love the idea. She really had no choice but to accept Adam's offer, however much she might be hurting on her own account because she couldn't convince him of her innocence.

With a little nod, she said, fighting to sound calm and decisive, 'Yes, all right, I agree, for my son's sake.'

Adam unfolded himself, stood up and leaned over the desk, until his face was only inches from her own. The nostrils on his impressive nose flared, and his eyes when they met hers were soft, like brown velvet. She could smell his aftershave. He told her quietly, 'I promise you won't regret it, Daisy. I'll do all I can for the boy and, of course, for you. It'll be a new start for all of us.'

He bent lower, and she knew that he was going to kiss her. Hairs stood up on the back of her neck. Her breathing quickened. Common sense told her to resist him, but her fast-beating heart belied common sense as she waited for his lips to touch hers. But they didn't. Instead of kissing her on the mouth, he parted her golden fringe with long fingers and brushed her forehead with his lips. 'For old times' sake and to seal our bargain,' he said in a slightly husky voice.

It was a chaste, cool kiss, free of any sexual or emotional overtones. A brotherly kiss, yet somehow more unnerving than the kiss on the mouth which she had been expecting—wanting! Making a tremendous effort she gathered herself together. 'Don't you think it would be more appropriate to shake hands?' she said sharply, proud of her steady voice. 'After all, we've entered into what amounts to a business arrangement, purely for Rupert's benefit.'

Adam straightened up and stared at her in surprise. 'Is that how you see it?' he asked. 'I thought we had much more going for us than a business arrangement. I thought we were beginning to understand each other and make friends at last, because we've agreed to disagree.'

'Then you thought wrong,' she said brusquely. 'You've made it perfectly plain ever since I arrived here that you accept me only as a colleague. Nothing we've said this afternoon alters the situation; you still have too many reservations about me.'

'And how do you suppose I'm to get to know Rupert better if you persist in putting up barriers? He'll sense that something is wrong between us,' he said in a suddenly hard voice.

'Oh, don't worry, Adam, I will act a part when the three of us are together. After all, you consider me a consummate actress, having lived a lie all these years. A little bit of play-acting for my son's benefit isn't going to try my skill at pretending.'

'*Touché*,' said Adam. His voice was bitter. 'If you can act a part, so can I. But oh, my dear Daisy, I wish things had been different between us.' And, with a nod, he turned on his heel and left the office.

CHAPTER SEVEN

AND so do I, thought Daisy as the door closed behind him. With all my heart I wish things had been different. Oh, Adam, if only your loyalty to Matthew didn't blind you to the truth.

Forget it, that's wishful thinking, she told herself sadly as she made a huge effort to concentrate on work for the rest of the afternoon and put the whole episode with Adam out of her mind. It wasn't easy, but she had just succeeded, and was in the middle of tackling the off-duty roster, when there was a tap at the door, and Matron, as elegantly gracious as ever, sailed into the office.

'Daisy, I bring good tidings,' she said, beaming a smile at Daisy as she sat down in the visitor's chair on the other side of the desk. She seemed in a particularly happy mood. 'Firstly, I've just heard from Jenny McClure that her mother's on the mend, so she will be back on duty next week. Which means, of course, that as from Monday you'll be able to return to your own office and put on your assistant matron's hat. Isn't that splendid news?'

'Oh, yes, that's marvellous,' Daisy agreed, but found, to her surprise, that she had to force a note of enthusiasm into her voice. How extraordinary; she should be delighted with the knowledge that she was returning to her own office, but in fact felt only a wave of regret at the thought of leaving the medical wing. Now why on earth did she feel like that? Certainly she would miss being in direct contact with the patients, but that alone couldn't be responsible for her reaction, surely?

The truth shook her as it dawned on her. It was Adam she was going to miss. For, although she would see him for a short while each day in Admin, it wouldn't be the same as working beside him and sharing in the intimate care of the patients, as she had done for the last few weeks on medical.

Common sense told her that it was ridiculous to feel like this after the words that had passed between them this afternoon, and the way they had parted. She ought to be glad that she would be seeing less of him at work, for the less she saw of him the better. It would make their peculiar relationship easier to handle.

She smiled at Matron, who was looking at her shrewdly, almost as if she was aware of the thoughts that had flashed through her mind. But, of course, that was nonsense; she couldn't possibly know how Adam had figured in them.

But there was no doubt that she had guessed at some of Daisy's thoughts for, after a moment, she said with a wry smile, 'Well, well, you sound rather less than enthusiastic about taking up the reins again as my assistant. I presume, indeed I hope, it's because you're going to miss the hands-on nursing you've been doing and not because you've got cold feet about returning to your senior position as assistant matron? It isn't that, Daisy, is it?' she asked, frowning slightly.

Daisy shook her head, surprised by Matron's suggestion. 'Certainly not,' she said firmly. 'Nothing was further from my thoughts.'

'Well, I'm glad you haven't any doubts. I know you were only in the job for a short while before acting as relief, and scarcely had time to get acclimatised, but you should be raring to get back to your proper post. After all, it was what you wanted, what you applied for, with all its privileges and responsibilities. And to make up for missing out on the day-to-day nursing you will have the opportunity to take part in the management and overall care of patients and the introduction of new ideas. Make no mistake, that's just as satisfying in its own way, and something you were looking forward to tremendously when you came for your interview.'

'And I still am, Matron; please don't doubt that,' said Daisy forcefully, wanting to make up for her earlier lack of enthusiasm. How could she have disappointed this kind, generous woman by sounding so lukewarm—the woman who had given her a chance to further her career? She felt cross with herself. 'But you are right about missing the practical nursing, Matron; that's why I sounded so unenthusiastic—just for a moment I really regretted having to leave the patients and staff here. I've so enjoyed the last few weeks, but I do want to get back to what I consider my real job as your assistant.'

'Good, I'm very pleased to hear it,' Matron replied, sounding relieved. 'And you've made a splendid job of stepping into the breach, but I need your support and enthusiasm back in Admin. We're going to be busier than ever now that we have outline planning permission for the new rheumatology extension. And *that's* my second bit of good news, Daisy. We have permission for the extension from the council, and I'm relying on input from both you and Adam for finalising the plans. It's going to be hard but exciting work for the three of us, so the sooner we get started the better. It'll be great fun, working on the plans together. I'm so looking forward to it.'

Her grey eyes sparkled and her usually pale olive skin flushed slightly as she put up a hand to smooth her already smooth chignon of gleaming chestnut hair. For once, she was a little less than perfectly composed, and was almost bubbling with scarcely suppressed excitement.

She gave Daisy a brilliant smile. 'Of course, it will mean putting in a lot of hours, my dear, which might encroach upon your free time. Will you mind that?' she asked.

'Not at all,' replied Daisy emphatically and without any hesitation. She was indeed excited by the prospect of working on the plans with her gracious employer, and with Adam too. She also wanted to dispel any lingering doubts that Matron might have about her enthusiasm to return to Admin. 'It will be a pleasure and a privilege to be involved in such a project. It must be every nurses' dream to plan a whole new nursing unit.'

'Oh, believe me, it is,' said Matron happily. 'I've built or extended at Featherston many times over the last few years, but I never lose the sense of achievement when the building is completed and the first patients are admitted. It's rather like being a midwife, and finding that in spite of assisting at any number of births every new baby is something of a miracle. And, talking of babies, I must get along to maternity. I missed them on the round this morning.'

She stood up and moved across the room, motioning Daisy, who out of courtesy had risen, back into her chair. 'I'll see myself out,' she said. 'I look forward to having you back in the office on Monday, Daisy, and getting cracking on those plans and other business.' She opened the door. 'And now I'll away and leave you to get on,' she added and, with a cheerful wave of her hand, she left the office.

Daisy would have liked to have time to mull over the news that Matron had brought, but she had only just left when there was a tap at the door, and Lisa Scott, her bright and efficient senior staff nurse, breezed in.

She gave Daisy a wide smile. 'Now that all the VIPs have gone I thought, if you're ready, we might get down to business and sort out notes for the report,' she said cheerfully.

'Of course, I'm ready,' Daisy told her, returning her smile and thinking how pleasant it was to deal with someone as uncomplicated as Lisa. 'Shoot.'

'Mrs Cambridge, complaining about her diet yet again. What are we going to do with her, Daisy? We've explained over and over that she's got to lose more weight before Mr Bonny will do her hip replacement.'

'What a pity she had visitors when Dr Torrence was doing his round. He might have been able to convince her.'

'I doubt it; even the charismatic Dr T would have been hard put to it to compete with her chocolates.'

'Don't say her husband is still smuggling in the forbidden chocolates?'

''Fraid so. Found a half-eaten box in her bedside locker.'

'Right, I'll go along in a minute and read her the riot act and confiscate them.'

'Rather you than me. She's going to be very cross; she wouldn't let me take them away.'

'That's my job; it's what I'm here for—to carry the can. Now, who's next?'

'Brian Thompson, poor chap, trying to come to terms

with his multiple sclerosis; he's very depressed; would you have a word?'

'Of course, if you think it would help.'

'I do; he has a lot of faith in you.'

'Sadly, in these situations, faith is not enough. I can only endorse what Dr Torrence and other medicos have told him about his condition.'

'Nevertheless, I'm sure you can reassure him. Perhaps you can persuade him that a remission is possible, or that the disease might slow down. I know you mustn't be over-confident, but he needs something to hang on to at present.'

'I'll certainly do my best. If only he would accept professional counselling, that might help him more than anything at this stage.'

'Perhaps it's worth suggesting again.'

'Yes, I might well do that. Anyway, I'll make a note in the report that he needs lots of reassurance at the moment. Now, who else have we got for special mention?'

'Colonel Snow; I've just changed his dressing. You'll be pleased to hear that his ulcer is clean at last. The Intrasite worked wonders as usual, clearing out the slough, so I've replaced it with an Opsite film, as prescribed by Dr T. With luck it should be granulating soon.

'And then there's Mrs Grantham. She's complaining of severe pain in her shoulder; the bruising's coming out now and is very extensive; I'm not surprised she's in pain, poor old thing. It's a miracle that she didn't break something when she fell. I've given her two DF118 tabs; I know they're quite strong, but she may need more tonight.'

'Well, she's written up for a repeat of DF118, PRN, so the night sister can decide if she needs anything.'

'Then that's the lot; all the others are as you saw them on the round with our Dr Torrence; no change.'

'Right, I'll get stuck into the report, and you get going, Lisa; it's time you were off duty.'

'OK, see you in the morning.'

She was on the way to the door when Daisy remembered that she had some news to pass on to her. 'Hang on a minute, Lisa; I've got some good news for you, which you can relay to the others. Jenny McClure will be back on Monday; her mother's much better.'

'Oh, super, I am pleased. She was so worried about her mother—at one time she didn't think she was going to make it. But we're all going to miss you, Daisy. It's been great working with you. Though I dare say you'll be glad to get back to Admin after slumming it down here for the past few weeks.'

'Well, I don't know about that; I'm going to miss you lot too, and the patients. Thanks for all the help and support you've given me, Lisa. It's been much appreciated. I couldn't have managed without you.'

'It's been a pleasure,' said Lisa, with a smile.

It was quiet in the office after Lisa had gone, and for a few moments Daisy sat very still, staring into space and thinking back over the afternoon. She had parted bitterly with Adam, and had almost hated him for a moment, and yet before Matron had broken the news about working together on the plans, and she had thought that she wouldn't be seeing much of him once she left Medical, she had been quite shaken.

There was so much about him that she admired. Had she been justified in labelling him patronising? Should she have blamed him for trying to find excuses for what he thought was her adulterous behaviour? Was he truly trying to understand her, and had he meant the excuses honestly and not as a sop to her conscience?

The questions hung unanswered in the air. She was unable to reach any conclusions. Impatiently, she mentally shook herself; now was not the time or the place to work out personal problems. She had work to do. Resolutely she started to write up the day report.

She finished just before six and handed over to Joy Kent, the most senior staff nurse on evening duty, and prepared to go off duty herself.

All she wanted to do now was to get home and talk to Rupert about their Saturday expedition, and break the news to him that Adam had suggested giving them a lift into town. Of course, he might turn down the offer, and want to go shopping with her alone, but she didn't think that was very likely. He had on one occasion hinted that it would be nice to have a man to help him choose his bike. 'You know, Mum,' he'd explained with surprising patience, obviously not wanting to hurt her feelings, 'because men know about gears and tyres and things,' and had added rather wistfully, 'Do you think Mr Hill would come with us if I asked him?'

But Daisy had squashed that idea. 'The Hills do quite enough for us without encroaching on their weekend when I'm off duty,' she'd said firmly.

And she was right about Rupert's response to Adam's offer. He made this quite plain when, having collected him from the Hills where he had had his tea, she passed the invitation on to him.

'Wow, that's brilliant,' he whooped happily, bouncing up and down. 'I like Dr Torrence.'

'You can't know that for sure, love; you only met him once, when he came to the bungalow before we moved in,' she said, trying gently to damp down his enthusiasm, afraid that he might be disappointed when he met Adam again.

Rupert opened his dark brown eyes in surprise and shook his head. 'No, I haven't, Mum,' he replied, to her astonishment. 'Only met him once, I mean. We often see him when we come home from school, and he always stops and speaks to us, and when we're playing football on the green he sometimes joins in. He's great. And anyway, he's an old friend of yours, and he knew my dad, so that makes him special, doesn't it?'

Daisy swallowed her astonishment and said feebly, 'Yes, I suppose it does.' It surprised her to think that Rupert had evidently given the matter of the old friendship some thought, and reached a positive conclusion about it. Adam must have made a tremendous impression at their meetings.

But why hadn't Adam told her that he'd been having conversations with her son? she wondered. He'd given the impression that he had no idea how Rupert was getting on, yet this was obviously not true, as he'd seen him on several occasions. Unless he thought that Rupert had told her that they had met. Or perhaps he considered that these meetings didn't count because they were casual, and there had been other children around, and therefore were not sigificant.

In fact, were they significant, or did they only seem so to her? Another unanswerable question, she thought irritably; life seemed to be full of them at the moment, making everything so complicated.

A little later, as she tucked Rupert up in bed, he said, 'You are glad, aren't you, Mum, that Dr Torrence is coming with us on Saturday?'

'Yes, of course I am,' she said quickly, breathing

hard at the thought of it as she bent to kiss his pink cheek. 'Very glad. Goodnight, love, sleep well.'

She left the room, quietly closing the door behind her, and made her way to the sitting-room, where she sat staring unseeingly at the television screen, deep in thought.

Glad. Yes, ludicrous as it was in the circumstances, she was glad about Saturday's outing. She couldn't help herself. Try as she might, she couldn't stem the rising tide of pleasure she felt as she contemplated being in Adam's company for several hours.

It was nonsense, of course, to be looking forward to being with him when she had so forcefully rejected the hand of friendship that he had held out that afternoon. She thought back over their discussion after the round, and was sorry that she had parted from him so bitterly. For, on reflection, she was sure that he hadn't meant to offend her by his arrogance. From his point of view, he had honestly tried to offer her a way out of the deadlock that existed between them. And, as he had pointed out, it was in Rupert's interest that they should be friends, and she couldn't quarrel with that.

All she could do was hope that she hadn't blown her chances for good with her refusal to accept the friendly kiss he had so casually brushed across her forehead. He had seemed genuinely hurt by her rejection. Well, if necessary, she was willing to eat humble pie if it would establish harmony between them and, if the opportunity arose, she would apologise for being so uncompromising.

She had almost succeeded in putting her muddled thoughts from her and turning her attention to the news, when there was a ring at the front doorbell. She looked at the clock. Just after nine. It must be Janice come round for a nightcap and a chat, as she did occasionally. Daisy sighed. Usually she welcomed her neighbour's company and the titbits of gossip she brought with her from the office where she worked part time, but tonight she would have preferred to be alone with her mixed-up thoughts. But Janice was a wonderful neighbour and Daisy put on a cheerful smile, prepared to give her a warm welcome.

She opened the door wide with a greeting on her lips, only to find that it wasn't Janice but Adam, revealed in a mixture of porch and moonlight.

Daisy gaped at him, taking in his tracksuit and trainers, though surprise robbed her of speech for a moment.

'Evening,' he said abruptly in his deep, rich baritone. He was unsmiling, serious. 'I hope I didn't startle you. May I come in, or is it too late for visitors?'

'No,' said Daisy, recovering her poise and trying to sound normal. 'I thought it might be somebody else.' She pulled the door wide open. 'Please come in.' What did he want, why had he come? He looked rather grim. Of course, not surprisingly, he was still angry with her for her rejection of him this afternoon.

He didn't move, but stayed planted four-square in the porch. 'No, I won't come in if you're expecting somebody else,' he told her firmly. 'But we need to talk some time, Daisy, before the weekend, and I don't mean in snatched moments at work.'

Daisy squashed a flutter of anticipation. 'Then please do come in,' she said evenly. 'I only thought it might be Janice from next door, but it's getting a bit late for her; she's not likely to come now.'

'Well, if you're sure.'

'Positive.'

'Right.' Adam stepped into the hall. Daisy was very conscious of his large, broad-shouldered presence, of the masculine smell of him as he brushed past her. He seemed to loom over her. 'I suppose Rupert's in bed?' he queried softly as he followed her into the sitting-room.

'Yes, why, had you hoped to see him?'

'No, as I said, it's you I wanted to see. I was out jogging—I try to do it in the evening, less people about—and I found myself up this way, and thought it might be as good a time as any to talk to you undisturbed.'

'Oh, really?' said Daisy sharply, feeling suddenly nervous. 'Please sit down.' She motioned to one of the armchairs by the fireplace. 'Would you like a drink? I can offer you whisky or wine, or a gin and tonic.'

'A whisky would be fine, thank you. Give me Dutch courage,' he replied, with a quirky, lop-sided smile, a hint of humour glinting for a moment in his sombre dark eyes.

Daisy gave him a surprised look. 'I can't imagine you needing Dutch courage,' she said as she poured a whisky for him and a gin and tonic for herself. She handed him his glass and then sat herself down in the armchair at the opposite side of the fireplace. 'You're too—too. . .'

'Patronising?' he supplied, with a faint grin, raising one eyebrow and staring hard back at her.

'No,' said Daisy, blushing as she realised that he was reminding her with gentle sarcasm of her accusation earlier in the day. 'Too confident, too self-assured.'

'Well, I'm neither at the moment,' he admitted, with a wry smile. 'In fact I hardly know where to begin.' He leaned forward in the chair, looking down at his glass as he rolled it between his long, lean hands.

Such nice, clever hands, thought Daisy, so competent; how strange to see him unsure of himself. She looked at his bent head, admiring the thick black hair with its occasional strands of silver glinting in the lamplight, and said in a rush, a little uncertainly, 'Is it about this afternoon, Adam? Because if it is I want to say that I'm sorry——'

'Don't talk nonsense,' he interrupted sharply as his head came up with a jerk and he looked straight into her eyes. 'You have nothing to be sorry about. You reacted quite naturally to my attempt to resolve matters between us. On reflection, I can see why you felt that I was being arrogant by finding reasons for your leaving Matthew, though I'd certainly no intention of being so.'

'I know; I realised that later.'

'Did you?' He sounded relieved, or perhaps it was hopeful. His eyes brightened a little.

'Yes. When I had time to think about it, I knew that you wouldn't deliberately set out to hurt me.'

'I'm grateful for that. You're right—it's the last thing I'd do. When I left your office this afternoon I thought that our fragile relationship was irrevocably damaged. You practically froze me out. I'm delighted to know that I was wrong.' A smile hovered round his previously stern mouth, and his expressive eyes suddenly grew warmer and almost tender as he looked across at her. 'So can we forget our misunderstanding and be friends?' he asked softly and, it seemed to Daisy, almost seductively. 'And not with you just playing a part for Rupert's sake, but because you mean it?'

Alarm bells sounded. He was taking too much for granted, too quickly. Much as she wanted his friendship she must not let this charismatic man take control and virtually brainwash her. She said, with all the calm and courage she could muster, 'Friends! Yes, Adam, we can be that. But do remember that, although I've accepted that you didn't mean to patronise me by inventing reasons for why I left Matthew, you mustn't think for one moment that I don't repudiate them whole-heartedly. Because I do, and you must accept that I do, and not try to persuade me to say otherwise. Persist, if you must, out of loyalty, in believing Matthew's story rather than mine, but don't expect me to change my story to please you, because I won't. We can be friends if you can come to terms with that.'

There was silence in the sitting-room, during which Daisy found herself holding her breath as she stared at him. Was Adam disappointed or angry because she hadn't capitulated completely? Was he going to refuse her terms of friendship, insist once again that Matthew, and only Matthew, had been telling the truth and hope to persuade her to water down her story?

He took a sip of whisky and continued to look at her over the rim of his glass. She returned his look unwaveringly, though inwardly she was quaking. What would she do if he decided against friendship on her terms? Could she possibly stay at the clinic if he was to try constantly to undermine her, directly or by innuendo?

Silently she cursed the fate that had brought her and the mature, charismatic Adam, to whom she was increasingly attracted, face to face after all these years. It would have been so much easier had she disliked him; she wouldn't then have hankered for his approval of her as a woman as well as a nurse.

They continued to watch each other warily, like two combatants sizing each other up before battle, then

Adam leaned forward and stretched out a hand. 'Friends,' he said quietly, 'on your terms.'

Daisy put her hand into his and felt it clasped in his large, reassuring one. She replied in a relieved, slightly breathless voice, 'Friends.'

There was a small silence as their eyes met, broken by a log slipping in the fire which Daisy had lit against the unexpected chill of the spring evening. It was a nice, homely sound. They smiled at each other a little self-consciously, and Adam pressed her hand gently and then released it. He raised his glass. 'To a long, happy and uncontentious friendship,' he said, 'both personal and professional.'

'I second that,' said Daisy, raising her own glass and touching his.

'Good.' He swallowed the last of his whisky and stood up. 'I'd best be off,' he declared with a rather tired smile, and Daisy thought, He's working too hard. 'All right if I pick you up about ten on Saturday?'

'Fine, thank you.'

'Perhaps we could take in a suitable film for Rupert in the afternoon?'

'That would be lovely; he'd like that. But please don't feel that you have to entertain us.'

'I don't feel that I *have* to do anything,' he assured her gently. 'I *want* to be involved with you both.'

Daisy's heart beat a little faster, but she frowned as she said, 'Adam, you do realise, don't you, that there's bound to be talk if the three of us go out together? You know what a hotline of gossip the grape-vine is.'

'Well, I don't mind if you don't, and I'm sure some people already know that we trained at the same hospital so it might be considered natural that we're friendly.' He grinned broadly. 'In fact, what could be more appropriate than that the assistant matron and the medical officer should get together?'

Daisy gave an uncertain little giggle and felt her cheeks redden. 'Yes, I suppose that's true. I haven't broadcast it exactly, but somebody recognised your hospital tie and my badge one day and assumed that we'd known each other when we were training, and I confirmed that we had.'

Adam's brown eyes gleamed with gold flecks in the firelight and his well-cut lips quirked at the corners. 'Then let's give the gossips a field day, and start on Saturday as we mean to go on, the three of us together. Let's give loving friendship a whirl.' He bent, kissed her gently on the cheek then pulled her to her feet and for the briefest of moments held her in his arms.

Daisy gave a trill of laughter, suddenly feeling that a weight had been lifted off her shoulders. She reached up and boldly brushed her soft lips across his. 'Yes,' she said, smiling into his eyes. 'Let's.'

She slept well that night, comforted and warmed by the thought that she and Adam had parted friends on terms with which they could both agree. It would have been wonderful, of course, if he had said that he had believed her story, but that was too much to hope for as yet. Perhaps as time went on she might convince him. Meanwhile she was happy with the compromise they had achieved this evening, and so, it seemed, was Adam, for he had kissed her again at the front door, a firm, satisfying kiss on her mouth. 'To seal our bargain of friendship,' he had murmured, before wishing her goodnight and jogging off into the moonlight.

CHAPTER EIGHT

THE next morning Daisy woke feeling refreshed after a dreamless sleep, aware that something pleasant had happened the night before. Of course. . . Adam had kissed her—a kiss of friendship, he'd said—and they had resolved their differences. All was well, and she would be seeing him on the wing in a few hours' time. Her thoughts raced along, propelled by her feeling of well-being. Life was wonderful. Rupert was settled and content, with an ever widening circle of friends, and loving every minute of living at Featherston. Free from anxiety, her heart soared. She was blissfully happy, the happiest she had been for months.

There were two more days in which to enjoy her hands-on nursing and Adam's frequent visits to the wing, though he would be off on Friday at a conference, and then it would be the weekend and their outing to Brighthelm for the longed-for bicycle. And after that her return to Admin and the satisfying prospect of working on the plans for the new rheumatology unit with Matron *and* Adam.

Her mood seemed to match the brilliant blue and gold of the April morning and she found herself singing a slightly off-key version of 'One Fine Day' from *Madam Butterfly* as she prepared breakfast for herself and Rupert.

'You sound happy, Mum,' he said as he came into the kitchen, starting off the day looking scrubbed and neat in his uniform. 'Is it because you're glad you're going back to being assistant matron?'

'Yes, I am, though I love the practical nursing too, but, as I told you yesterday, we're going to be working on the plans for the new unit, and that's very exciting.'

'You mean the rheuma. . .something unit.'

'Rheumatology, yes.'

'Mr Hill says a lot of that's to do with aching bones and muscles and things, and is going to mean a lot more work for his physio department and he hopes that the powers that be will give him more help.'

Daisy laughed. 'I'm sure that will be taken care of and Mr Hill will get more physiotherapists for his department when the time comes.'

Rupert frowned over a mouthful of cereal and asked thoughtfully, 'Mum, are you one of the powers that be?' He gave her a very direct look from under his long lashes, his brown eyes as dark as his father's—or Adam's, she thought.

'Well, yes,' said Daisy slowly, answering carefully, not having thought about the matter before and not wanting to give the boy the wrong impression. 'I suppose I am, since I help Matron make decisions.'

'Wow!' said Rupert, with a wide grin. 'You *are* very important, aren't you?'

'Everyone's important who works at the clinic, from the ladies in the kitchen to Dr Torrence as medical officer. We work as a team at Featherston. Don't ever forget that, Rupert; teamwork is everything.'

'OK, I won't forget.' He smiled cheekily as he spooned up the last of his cereal. 'But I still think it's brill, you being a VIP.'

Daisy returned his grin. 'You little horror,' she said, giving him an affectionate push towards the kitchen door. 'Go and get your gear from your room or you'll be late for the minibus and I'll be late for work, and I've got a busy day ahead of me.'

A little later, Rupert safely on the bus, she set off for the clinic, walking briskly along the lane, revelling in the warm spring sunshine but eager to get on duty.

She experienced a fresh tingle of happiness as she relished the thought that soon she would be caught up in the day's events on the wing, and as a bonus would be seeing Adam. Adam who had kissed her so warmly last night—though, she reminded herself, it had been a kiss of friendship, nothing more, and she must never forget that. And it was just as well that friendship was all that she wanted, for somewhere in England, as he had told her on that one occasion when he had let the barriers down, he had a long-lost love whom nobody, not even his partner in Africa, had been able to supplant.

Well, that was all right with her, and the knowledge didn't even dent her feeling of well-being this morning. After all, she assured herself, she wasn't in love with the man; she just found him a joy to work with and was content with his friendship.

The wing, when she arrived, was like any ward in any hospital at that time of the morning, and a sort of organised chaos reigned. In fact, everyone was going about their business purposefully, though to the uninitiated it must have looked as if a bomb had hit the place, and nobody knew what they were doing or where they were going.

There seemed to be a lot of people milling around. Breakfast trays were still being removed from rooms, and laundry trolleys were parked outside doors where beds were being made. Nurses were flitting up and down the corridor to the sluice-room with bedpans, bottles and commodes, and a staff nurse was busy at the medicine trolley loading up the day's supply from the secure drug cupboard.

Daisy bade everyone in sight a cheerful good morning and went into her office to read the report, which, as she was not on duty until nine, had been handed over by the night sister to Joy Kent, the senior staff nurse on duty.

There was nothing spectacular in it. Mrs Cambridge was still complaining of being starved, and had tried to wheedle a biscuit out of the new junior on duty. Brian Thompson had needed much reassurance before eventually going to sleep. Mrs Grantham's shoulder had been very painful during the night, and she had been given a further two tablets of DF118. Mr Hall, query gastric ulcer, in for investigation, had complained of pain in his stomach and had been given Mist Mag Trisil, with good settling effect, though he had vomited a little on waking this morning. No sign of blood in vomit, but same saved and labelled for laboratory inspection, in the sluice-room. The three patients to be discharged today had all been awake early and were raring to go. Otherwise nothing had changed since the previous evening's report.

When she had finished reading Daisy began gathering up the post, which had been piled on her desk, to distribute on her round. She was nearly finished when there was a tap at the half-open door, and at her invitation to, 'Come in,' Adam entered. She hadn't been expecting him till later and, to her chagrin, at the unexpected sight of him her pulse started racing and her heart seemed to leap in her breast. This is ridiculous, she thought; he's just a friend, remember, an old friend whom you've known for ages, since he was a green, sometimes over-exuberant young houseman. You mustn't let the mature, responsible man that he's become bowl you over.

'Good morning,' she said, in a studiously calm voice. 'I'm surprised to see you so early.'

He gave her a brilliant smile. He looked different today, she thought—just like she felt: very vibrant, very alive. It was as if he was as happy as she was. It must be the warm spring weather and the brilliant sunshine. She could almost feel the energy pulsing from him. He was looking incredibly handsome and masculine in a light-weight fawn suit, crisp white shirt and an unexpectedly flamboyant, multicoloured tie that seemed to match his mood.

'*Hello*, and how are *you* on this brilliant spring morning?' he drawled in a deep, teasing sort of voice as he beamed at her across the room. His dark eyes were full of laughter. He said, with a chuckle, 'You know, you look lovely with the sun shining on you and that ridiculous little lace cap perched on your daffodil-yellow hair. A real sunshine girl. Do you feel as good as you look?'

'How very poetic; I'm f-fine,' she stammered a little breathlessly, giving a low, almost shy laugh, startled by the teasing and unexpected warmth of his greeting. 'And you?'

'Oh, I'm fine too,' he said, and smiled as if something amused him. 'Never better.' He crossed the room and stood looking intently down at her as she sat behind her desk, her hands full of the morning post. In a very soft voice he murmured, 'And if I'm poetic, Daisy, it's because I'm feeling in that sort of mood this morning.

I'm so very happy on account of our getting our difficulties ironed out last night. It's great to be friends again.'

'Oh, Adam, it is,' she breathed.

They stared at each other a moment longer. His deep-set eyes caught the sunlight and glowed a chestnut-brown as he leaned closer over the desk. Daisy thought, He's going to kiss me. Her cheeks burned, her pulse raced even faster. Her lips parted slightly. She shivered as a feeling of *déjà vu* washed over her. This had happened before. Adam had leaned over the desk, and she had thought then that he was going to kiss her, but he hadn't—well, not properly. He had given her a cool, enigmatic kiss on the forehead. Was he planning the same thing this time?

Pride made her pull herself together. No way was that going to happen again, for, much as she would like to feel his lips on hers, she was not going to give him the chance to kiss her on the mouth or anywhere else; she would give herself and her feelings away if he did, and she knew that she mustn't do any such thing and risk spoiling their new relationship. She must see to it that they remain just the good friends that he had suggested until he—what? Until he believed in her absolutely and stopped yearning for his long-lost love, whispered a little voice in the back of her head.

She wouldn't be satisfied with anything less than total commitment from the man she loved.

The man she loved!

There! She had admitted it to herself at last; she wasn't just drawn to Adam, she didn't want him just as a friend—she was in love with him! It was a relief to have acknowledged it finally. She loved the way he had matured, grown in stature, physically and intellectually.

She loved the way that he responded to his patients, with warmth and understanding. But he must never know the way she felt, not until he was ready. She mustn't frighten him off by being too intense.

She took in a deep breath, forced her eyes away from his, pushed her chair back, and with an immense effort smiled calmly up at him. She said briskly, 'And what brings you here so early, Adam? Is there anybody particularly that you wanted to see?'

If her sudden briskness surprised him, he didn't show it, but straightened himself up from the desk and sat down in the visitor's chair. He gave her an amused, speculative look, and for an uneasy moment she wondered if he knew how she truly felt about him, but immediately discarded the idea as ridiculous. Perceptive he might be, but a mind-reader he was not.

As quickly as it had come, his amused, speculative look vanished, and to her surprise he said with sudden quiet seriousness, 'Well, I wanted to see *you*, Daisy, to make quite sure that the way we took leave of each other last evening wasn't just a figment of my imagination, and we really did part good friends.' He looked at her thoughtfully for a moment and then smiled and added lightly, 'And apart from that I thought I'd pop in and say goodbye to the patients for discharge, if that's all right with you.'

'Of course; that'll be fine; feel free.' She felt reassured and pleased by his admission of uncertainty over what had passed between them last night. It was rather endearing that he had confessed to feeling unsure of himself for once. She didn't know whether he had been about to kiss her moments before, but it was quite clear from what he had said that what he wanted most from her was friendship. Well, that was what he would get; that suited her for the present. She gave him a dimpled smile. 'And are you convinced,' she asked teasingly, 'that we did part friends last night?'

Adam said softly, 'Oh, yes, I think you've made it perfectly clear that you feel as I do; you've set my mind at rest on that score. I'm delighted that we're both on the same wavelength, Daisy.' His eyes were full of gentle humour as he gave her a quirky, whimsical smile.

Daisy smiled a little uncertainly back at him, but said firmly, 'Yes, I'm glad too,' still not too sure what he was really thinking. Were his words as innocent as they sounded, or was he teasing her? Again she asked herself, Had he read her mind, did he know or suspect anything of her true feelings, had her manner given her away?

A half-smile still on his lips, Adam continued to watch her for a moment, then stood up, squared his broad shoulders and, becoming all at once the doctor, said briskly, 'And now I'd best be off and say farewell to these lucky people who are going home. Don't come with me; you're busy. I'll see you later when I come in to check on the new admissions.'

With an effort, Daisy became her professional self too, and, matching his briskness, said, 'Right, but before you go, Adam, will you sign this lab form? Mr Hall vomited this morning so I'm sending a specimen for examination as per your instructions.'

'Any visible blood in it?' he asked as he put his signature to the form.

'No, and no other signs of an internal bleed. Pulse volume good, respirations and blood-pressure near normal, temperature slightly raised last night.'

'Well, we'll wait for the results of the barium tests and so on, and take it from there. Perhaps our Mr Hall is suffering from a long-term, low-grade chronic stomach infection,' he said thoughtfully as he handed back the form. 'Though his physical history reads like a typical gastric ulcer.'

'Yes, it does,' confirmed Daisy. 'But I don't think he has the temperament. He's rather a calm, usually cheerful individual, not agitated as gastrics often are.'

'Well, we'll just have to wait on events.' He strode to the door, turned, and gave her a lovely, tender smile that set her heart thumping. 'See you later,' he said, lifting a hand in salute.

'See you,' she murmured as with unusually clumsy fingers she shuffled the post into order. Then, a few minutes later, she followed him out into the corridor, looking, as always, cool, calm and collected.

The next couple of hours were hectic, and she had no time to ponder over Adam's teasing, almost exultant behaviour earlier. She supervised the discharge of the patients who were going home, and accepted a flurry of grateful thanks and small gifts for herself and other staff. As soon as they were gone nurses and domestics whipped into the empty rooms to change bedding and clean lockers and generally make things ready for the new patients being admitted later.

The first to arrive was an elderly lady, Mrs Mornington. She was bent nearly double and unable to walk unaided, and spent her life between bed and wheelchair. She was suffering from osteoporosis, which had affected her spinal column with a typical curvature. In addition she was fighting chronic bronchitis, emphysema and arthritis. There wasn't a lot that could be done for her, except to keep her comfortable and free from pain with medication and careful nursing and perhaps physiotherapy. She had come to the clinic chiefly to give her caring relatives a rest for a few weeks and the staff's job was to make her stay a happy one.

Daisy went to the new patient's room to see her safely installed and to reassure her and her daughter, Mrs Parsons, who had accompanied her. In spite of her disabilities, Mrs Mornington was a pleasant, still well-groomed old lady with an attractive hairdo and carefully applied make-up. She was beautifully dressed in a beige wool suit and cream silk blouse. When she was sitting down or in bed, her curvature was hardly noticeable, and she managed to look very elegant and chic.

Mrs Parsons was far more anxious than her mother about her stay in Featherston Hall, and was clearly feeling guilty about leaving her at the clinic while she went on holiday.

'But it's a holiday for Mrs Mornington too,' comforted Daisy. 'She can go along to the sitting-room whenever she likes and meet some of our other residents. If she's a card player, there's always someone anxious to make up a four for bridge or whist, and partners are always in demand for Scrabble or chess or dominoes. And if she doesn't want to watch television alone in her room she can go to the TV room or just go and have a chat with someone. In other words, she will always have company if she wants it.'

'Well, I never imagined it would be like this!' exclaimed Mrs Parsons, looking much relieved. 'I won't feel so bad about leaving her now.'

The next new patient to be admitted, just before lunch, was a tall blond sixteen-year-old called Tony Pascal, who was recovering from mononucleosis.

'It's commonly known as glandular fever,' Daisy explained to Karen Keen, a young pre-student nurse working as a junior auxiliary, whom she had detailed to help Staff Nurse Joy Kent, who was specialling the three new admissions. 'Tony's father, a widower, is a naval officer and has arranged for us to look after his son while he's away at sea.

'Now, the most important factor in recovery from glandular fever is rest, good food and reassurance. It's a very debilitating condition, and at present Tony has a chest infection, for which he's having an antibiotic. Staff Nurse will look after his medication and diet and do his TPR chart, while you do the other chores and help keep him cheerful. Since you're near to him in age you should have things in common, which is why I hope you'll be most useful in helping to special him.

'But remember, Karen, you'll be on duty at all times, so be sensible when you deal with him; don't let personal feelings run away with you. Any problems, speak to Staff or to me.'

The third admission didn't arrive till after lunch. She was Sally Rider, a young woman of twenty-two, suffering from anorexia nervosa, who had been referred by her desperate GP for care and such treatment as might be possible. She was very thin, underweight, depressed, withdrawn, yet agitated at the same time.

'You two are going to have your work cut out looking after this young woman,' Daisy said to Joy and Karen, when they reported to her after they had settled the newcomer in her room. 'She'll be tricky to deal with. Persuading her to eat will, of course, be the main problem, though at least she has consented to come into the clinic for help. But we'll wait till Dr Torrence has seen her before deciding on a line of action. We'll see whether he can come up with any brilliant ideas.' And if anyone can, it'll be Adam, she thought.

But she was wrong about that, because when he had seen Sally and Daisy asked what they could do for her he said tersely, 'Not a lot unless she fully co-operates.'

He had arrived to do his round in the same delightfully carefree mood that had intrigued her that morning, but by the time they returned to her office after he had examined the three new patients that mood had deserted him and he was sad and furiously angry.

He said savagely, as they sat down and he accepted the cup of tea that Daisy poured for him, 'God, I could throttle these people who make such a fetish of being slim. They do such incredible harm to young, impressionable girls, and, for that matter, older people too. And I'm not talking about real obesity, which is a disease in itself, but the people who make everyone feel bloody guilty if they're carrying a pound extra weight. All those waif-like girls in adverts perpetuate the myth.' He looked at her with bleak eyes. 'Oh, Daisy, what are we going to do for this young woman?'

She shook her head helplessly. 'I don't know, Adam; I was hoping you would come up with something.'

'Would that I could. But, as you know, these anorexics are the most difficult of patients because basically they don't want to do the one thing that will make them better, which is to eat. I'm limited as to what I can do. I can start her on chlorpromazine, if we can get her to accept it; it may calm her a little and help her gain weight. I can refer her for psychotherapy, which may help, and call in a dietician to plan a light but nourishing diet. But when it comes down to it, it depends on getting her to eat, and that, my dear Daisy, is mainly a nursing problem.'

He gave her a hard, speculative look from hooded

eyes, as if he wasn't really seeing her, and shrugged, running long fingers through his thick black hair with its grey flecks in a gesture of frustration that she well remembered.

'Of course, I could try nasal feeding if she would accept it, but I'm loath to suggest it at the moment; it might frighten her off. Poor, screwed-up kid, isn't she pathetic? All skin and bones and anxiety. We *must* do something to help her. She's going to deteriorate rapidly. We might even lose her if we don't come up with something damned quick. She's a very ill girl.'

He was terribly depressed because he felt so helpless. Daisy longed to say something to cheer him. Tea and sympathy was about all she had to offer. What a dear, compassionate man he was. She looked across at him, unable to conceal the love and admiration in her eyes. But he didn't notice; he was staring unseeingly into his empty teacup.

She said quietly, 'Well, you have thought of something, Adam—the chlorpromazine and the psychotherapy. I think we should start them as soon as possible. I don't know that a special diet is necessary; if we can just get her to have liquids or solids in minute quantities in any form that she will accept it'll be a breakthrough, and that's what we should concentrate on first.'

'You'll have her specialled?' he said sharply, looking up from his contemplation of his empty cup.

'Of course. In fact all three of the new patients are to be specialled by Joy Kent and our bright young pre-nursing student Karen Keen. The very fact that she's young and pretty should help both Sally and Tony Pascal.'

Adam managed a tight smile. 'Well, I don't know

how Sally will react, but I'm sure it will do young Tony the world of good to have a pretty girl of near enough his own age around. By the way, you will remind your nurses that Sally mustn't be left alone when having food or taking medicine, so that she doesn't have the opportunity to dispose of them, won't you?'

'Certainly,' she said firmly, smothering a moment's irritation that he thought it necessary to remind her of something so basic, then reminded herself that it was only his concern that made him do so. 'If you agree, I think we'll go for minuscule quantities of food and drink that she might find palatable, at frequent intervals, but we won't press her too much at first, and of course we'll chart her food and fluid intake.'

'Fair enough, but get something—anything—into her as soon as possible,' he said urgently. 'I'll write her up for the chlorpromazine, which she can start as soon as you get it up from Pharmacy, and I'll get in touch with Robin Brown, the senior psychiatrist at St Francis, to sort out some psychotherapy for her. I'll ask him to come or send someone to do an assessment as a matter of urgency.'

'That'll be great, thank you. Now what about young Tony Pascal?'

'We'll keep him on the antibiotic as his chest is still congested, and press fluids. And, of course, his temperature, pulse and respirations should be recorded on a BD morning and evening chart.

'Give him all the tender loving care that you can. He needs that, poor lad, as he seems to have been deprived of any female attention since his mother died. There's not much else one can do for him, except prevent him from getting bored. Perhaps your young, pretty nurse will do that. We'll do another blood test next week and see how things are shaping up, but at least his prognosis is good, given time, unlike young Sally's,' he said, grim-faced, eyes bleak again. He didn't seem to be able to get the young woman out of his mind.

'Right; and what about Mrs Mornington, Adam? Anything special in mind for her?'

'Ah, Mrs Mornington,' he said, handing over his cup for a refill, his grim expression softening a little. 'What a grand old lady she is. It's ironic, isn't it, that, in spite of her years, we *can* do something to help her? A little gentle physiotherapy, I think; it might improve those painful joints, and improve her chest condition, and also make her feel that we're taking an interest in her—very reassuring, especially when you get older. Her morale is good, but it can always do with a boost. Besides, she deserves it.

'We also might try to treat her chronic bronchitis and emphysema a little more effectively while she's with us, so let's run a few tests—blood, lung function and sputum. She's on a good bronchodilator inhaler, but a little oxygen each day wouldn't come amiss—might make her more comfortable. I'll write her up for a cylinder.' His eyes looked less bleak, and he actually smiled. His spirits appeared to have lifted somewhat. Daisy heaved a sigh of relief as she smiled back.

'That was a heartfelt sigh. What was it in aid of?'

Daisy said, with a rather self-conscious chuckle, 'I'm pleased to see you looking a little less fraught.'

'Fraught? Did I look fraught?'

'Yes, over Sally Rider.'

'Oh,' he said, with a half-humorous smile. 'Was I so obviously breaking a basic rule about not getting involved with one's patients?'

'Yes, but I believe that any good doctor or nurse

sometimes does get involved. I don't think you can help it.'

'My sentiments exactly. It's nice to know that you share them.'

'I do.'

There was a moment's silence and Adam stared at her intently. 'And you actually cared how I felt?' he asked in a low, almost surprised voice.

'Yes.' She bent her head to avoid looking directly at him. 'I didn't like to see you so sad, though I understood why,' she said softly.

'I'm glad about that,' he murmured. Slowly he stretched out a hand and lifted her chin until her eyes met his. 'Do you really care about me, Daisy?'

She caught her breath. She felt helpless as she allowed her eyes to meld with his. In a voice hardly above a whisper she said, 'Of course I do, Adam; we're old friends.'

'Only old friends?'

'Yes; it's what you wanted, isn't it?'

His voice was very husky and deep as he confessed, 'I'm not sure. We're only a step away from——'

The telephone shrilled insistently. Adam dropped his hand from her chin, pulled a face and muttered something rude. Daisy blinked, took a trembling breath and, with a little *moue* of disappointment and a rueful smile, glanced from Adam to the jangling phone. Making a gesture of apology, she picked up the receiver with a hand that shook slightly and, clearing her throat, said sharply, 'Medical wing, Sister Marchment speaking.' Something was said at the other end of the line and Daisy replied in a staccato sort of voice, 'Yes, he's here; I'll hand you over.' She put her hand over the mouthpiece. 'It's Larry,' she said in a low voice. 'He's in Surgical and wants a word, sounds a bit agitated.'

Adam frowned, shrugged, and took the instrument from her. 'What's the problem, Larry?' he asked.

Daisy heard Larry's muffled voice saying something, then Adam said, 'Right, carry on with what you're doing; I'll be there in a few minutes.' He stood up and gave Daisy the ghost of a smile. 'Sorry about this. Problems with a cholecystectomy performed yesterday, so regretfully I've got to go.' His eyes, almost black, bored into hers, momentarily holding her captive again. 'But don't forget where we were at,' he added, 'because I won't.'

'Nor I,' she promised breathlessly, staring up at him towering over her.

He swooped down, leaned across the desk and this time kissed her swiftly, firmly, tenderly on the lips. 'That, Daisy, love, is on account,' he said softly with a gentle smile, and turned and made for the door.

Daisy, rendered silent by the suddenness of his kiss, touched her lips where his had touched them and watched him disappear through the doorway into the corridor. He didn't look back.

Bemused, she sat at her desk reflecting on what had happened. She could hardly believe it. There had been nothing 'just friendly' in his kiss or the expression in his eyes; both had been full of restrained passion. It had almost been a declaration, a lover's kiss, and somehow inevitable. But could it really have been? Was that what he'd meant? Was he in love with her, or was she reading too much into that kiss? All sorts of thoughts raced through her mind. And if he was saying that he was in love with her, was he admitting that he now believed her story rather than Matthew's? Or didn't that enter into his thinking?

He had agreed to the rules of friendship that she had laid down, but he didn't know that, in her own mind, she wanted more from him if they were to go further. Not that he had seemed to want anything more than friendship until now, and maybe he wasn't really saying that he was in love with her, though he had intimated as much.

He couldn't know that she expected him to have complete faith in her, believe her account of why she had left Matthew without question, before she would ever accept his love. But it was almost as if he did know that, had guessed at how she felt, for that was what his kiss and the way he had looked at her, his whole manner today, had seemed to imply. Perhaps he *was* telling her that he believed in her utterly, loved her utterly.

A tremulous wave of pleasure and breathless happiness washed over her. Surely Adam loved her, and that was what his kiss must have meant? It was unbelievable and wonderful, and she wished that she could tell him so, but there was nothing she could do about it at the moment. Duty had called before she could respond to him. Did he know, or had he realized, how she felt, or was he not sure? Would he ring her tonight, or visit, or wait till Saturday to discuss what had happened?

Wondering, she stared into space.

She would have liked to dwell on that swift and satisfying kiss, but sounds from the corridor penetrated, reminding her that she was on duty on the busy medical wing. With a great sigh, she resolutely pushed her racing thoughts aside, knowing that she must concentrate on work. She pulled the patient-card index towards her and began to write up the notes of the round. This, and writing the report, and talking to staff and patients, kept her occupied until she went off duty.

She daydreamed about Adam and his kiss as she walked up the lane from the clinic in the mellow evening sunshine, but Rupert, seeming so independent lately, required all her attention when she got home, and she had no time to dwell on her private thoughts.

It pleased her immensely that he came charging over from the centre green, where he was playing with his friends, directly he saw her. He was bubbling over with chatter about school and the forthcoming visit to Brighthelm on Saturday.

They went into the bungalow together. He was thrilled by Adam's suggestion that they go to see a film, for apparently there was Disney's latest offering on at one of the cinemas and he badly wanted to see it.

'But we will get my bike first, won't we?' he asked anxiously.

'Of course, love; that's our priority,' Daisy reassured him.

He gave her a beaming smile that touched her heart. 'That's all right, then,' he said happily, and added inconsequentially, 'Isn't Dr Torrence nice, Mum? I do like him.'

'Yes,' said Daisy calmly, battening down her raging emotions. 'Very nice.'

They had supper and watched a nature programme until just before nine o'clock, when Rupert went off to bed and Daisy settled down to try and concentrate on the news. But Adam was there all the time, in the back of her mind. Would he ring? Or would he suddenly turn up on her doorstep? If he did, what would he say? What *could* he say?

At eleven o'clock, just as she had given up hope of hearing from him and was about to go to bed, he rang.

'Daisy,' his familiar, warm, deep voice throbbed in her ear as soon as she picked up the receiver.

'Adam, I'm so glad you called,' she murmured, not caring that she sounded so eager, her breath coming raggedly. 'I wondered if you would.'

'Did you doubt it?'

'I couldn't be sure; you didn't say.'

'There was no question of letting this evening pass without seeing you or at least speaking to you after. . .' he hesitated for a moment '. . .what happened between us today. I simply had to hear your voice. We've so much to say to each other. I couldn't ring earlier; I've been busy all evening with one emergency or another, and I wanted to get everything sorted before going to this conference tomorrow. Of course if I damn well weren't on call I'd be with you right now,' he added with feeling.

'There's nothing wrong on the med wing, is there?' she asked at once, alarmed, her thoughts, even at this very private and personal moment, turning to her patients.

He laughed abruptly. 'No, it was Surgical and Maternity.'

'Thank goodness.'

'Very partisan,' he said drily.

'Of course; what else should I be?' It was a rhetorical question to which she didn't expect an answer. She hesitated. For some reason she felt incredibly nervous. She cleared her throat and tried to make her voice sound even and matter-of-fact, but there was a slight tremor in it as she asked, 'And what did you want to say to me, Adam?'

He didn't speak at once, and when he did his voice was velvet-soft, firm and pitched very deep. 'I wanted to tell you that I love you, Daisy, and I want to care for you and cherish you always.'

The words, softly spoken as they were, seemed to explode in her ear. What was he saying? Love! Cherish! She froze and stared unseeingly at a bowl of daffodils on a side-table. Time stood still. All the breath seemed to have been knocked out of her body by his words. She hadn't known quite what he would say, but she hadn't expected this, not this bald statement of love, not this promise to cherish. She had thought that he might refer teasingly, though tenderly, to the kiss, use it as a stepping-stone towards something more serious in the future, had thought that he might flirt with her a little — but not declare himself the way that he had, almost as if he was making a proposal of marriage.

Speech deserted her.

'Daisy, are you all right?'

'Yes, but I. . . I. . . I've got to go; Rupert's calling.'

Slowly, automatically, she replaced the receiver in its cradle, and gazed round the silent room. In a strange way, she was glad that Adam had not been able to call in person. She had to have time to think alone, to come to terms with the fact that he loved her.

CHAPTER NINE

DAISY sank down into an armchair and gazed into the depths of the glowing log fire.

Yes, she definitely needed time to think! Time to get over the shock of actually hearing Adam say, 'I love you,' in his rich, deep, drawling voice which had made the fine, golden-blonde hairs on her arms and the back of her neck quiver; time to mull over and savour the words that in moments had turned her world upside-down. 'I want to care for you and cherish you always.'

The word 'cherish' spun slowly round in her mind. What a wonderful word; it made her feel safe, comforted, protected. And surely he wouldn't have said that if he was still in love with someone else? He wouldn't have said it unless he trusted her implicitly, would he? Would he, could he? No. Adam was an honourable man. There was no need to ask him to explain his other love, for he had clearly, at last, put that love behind him. He didn't need to spell it out for her; she would never press him to tell her the whole story.

And there couldn't possibly be any need any longer to question whether he believed her story about how she had parted from Matthew. He wouldn't have declared himself in love with her if he'd still had doubts. She couldn't be mistaken; his faith in her seemed implicit in what he had said, and the way he had said it. He believed in her now.

Adam cherished her and loved her, and would take

care of her and Rupert. It was incredible but true. He had said as much. She ached to see him, to put her arms round him, and tell him that she loved him too, that she would cherish him in return.

For a long time she sat in front of the dying embers of the fire, going over and over his words, hearing again the infinitely tender tone in his voice as he'd spoken them. She pictured his thin, handsome face, the deep-set, dark, enigmatic eyes above the lean cheeks, the aristocratic nose and firm chin, and well-cut, firm lips just waiting to kiss her. She could smell the masculine scent of him, and almost feel his long, sinewy, sensitive, clever hands caressing her gently but surely as he made love to her.

She knew that he would be a passionate lover. A passionate but considerate lover. And she knew, too, that she would return his love with a wild, abandoned sort of passion, a passion that she had kept battened down for years. Her very loins quivered in anticipation.

Arms crossed over her bosom, she hugged herself with gleeful delight as she gave rein to her sensuous thoughts. It had been such a long, long time since she had felt the warmth of a man's arms about her and felt a hard body pressed against her own in an ecstasy of loving. The thought of making love to Adam, the sophisticated, dedicated man of medicine whom she had known, and yet not really known, for so long, almost took her breath away. She felt she could burst with happiness as she sat on in front of the now dead fire and daydreamed.

The little silver clock on the mantelpiece, a gift from Aunt Mary, struck midnight.

With a jerk, Daisy brought herself back to reality. She stood up and stretched, switched off the lights, and with a sigh of pure happiness took herself off to bed to dream some more and make plans for the weekend.

She and Adam would talk again on Saturday after their visit to Brighthelm. They would have a long, intimate discussion, and seal their love with long, intimate kisses. Her heart thumped at the thought. She would invite him to supper; it would be a fitting end to what was going to be a wonderful day. A day with Adam *and* her darling Rupert.

Rupert! Her heart missed a beat, a pulse drummed at her temple. How would he react to her having a much closer relationship with Adam? Why on earth hadn't she thought of this before?

She stared into the darkness, hardly daring to breathe. How could she have overlooked Rupert's feelings? True, he had made it clear that he liked Adam very much. He even seemed to admire him; but was that enough? He had been thrilled that Adam was coming with them to choose his bike—but was that enough to prepare him to accept the fact that his mother was in *love* with the charismatic Dr Torrence? Supposing he resented him, was unwilling to share her with him? And if or when Adam proposed marriage, would Rupert receive him happily as a stepfather? Would he?

Doubts crowded in on her. In moments, her happiness seemed to drain away, leaving her feeling cold and hollow. She lay stiff and rigid with anxiety, knowing that her son held the key to her future with Adam in his small hands, for she would never, ever do anything to make him unhappy.

Then quite suddenly, unexpectedly, a wave of hope and reason washed over her. Why shouldn't Rupert welcome Adam into a closer relationship? No one could be more suitable than Matthew's old friend. Rupert himself had said that Adam was special, and some instinct had drawn them together. And he *was* special. He had made it clear that he already felt emotionally involved with Rupert, and they had certainly formed a rapport at their first meeting.

Adam had virtually offered to be his role model, a father figure, and Rupert was ripe to accept one; he had shown that very obviously since moving to Featherston.

Slowly, very slowly, Daisy's fears began to fade, and she began to feel that all was going to be well. The two people she loved best in the world would love and respect each other. It might take a little while for Rupert to come to terms with the situation, but surely it was inevitable in the end that he would? And they had all the time in the world for a relationship to build up slowly and gently; there would be no harassment, no rush.

Yes, all was going to be well.

Unutterably weary after all the emotional ups and downs, but at last reassured, she closed her eyes, gave a huge sigh of relief, turned on her side, and fell quickly into a dreamless sleep.

Her fears laid to rest, engulfed by a wave of euphoria in anticipation of spending Saturday with Adam and an exuberantly happy Rupert, Daisy sailed through a frantically busy Friday at work. She was so hard-pressed, with all sorts of minor emergencies to attend to, that only occasionally did she have time to think, with a warm, almost overpowering glow of happiness, of Adam away at his conference.

It was one of the busiest days they had had on Medical for a long time, and it was also the warmest, like a summer's day, rather than a late spring one, with brilliant sunshine streaming in through the open windows. By mid-afternoon the patients were fractious, the bed-bound longing to be outside in the shady courtyard with the lucky convalescents, and the staff flagging. Firmly but gently she chivvied them all along, lent wings by her own blissful happiness. She organised ice-cold drinks for the patients who were allowed them, and for the staff and visitors, which perked everyone up.

And towards the end of the afternoon, after a long talk with Brian Thompson and his wife, she managed to persuade them to accept expert counselling to help them come to terms with his multiple sclerosis, and felt that she had done a good job.

Before going off duty she even achieved the minor miracle of starting Sally Rider on her chlorpromazine and getting her to take a couple of mouthfuls of a low-fat drink which, amazingly, the emaciated girl had fancied. Quite a breakthrough. Adam would be pleased, she thought, with an inward glow of delight.

Lying in bed later that night, waiting for sleep to come, she wondered, with a wry smile, who was looking forward most to the following day, she or her eight-year-old son. And what about Adam? Was he too looking forward to tomorrow's outing with such joy? She knew with absolute certainty that he would be. And on this delightful conclusion she drifted into sleep, and dreamt in a hazy manner of Adam and Rupert but not, this time, of Matthew.

Saturday had a touch of magic about it from the start.

Rupert woke early, as if it were Christmas morning,

bubbling over with happiness in anticipation of buying his first bicycle.

'May I come in with you, Mum?' he asked softly after tapping at her door.

He hadn't wanted to do that for ages.

'Of course you can, darling. Come on; pull back the curtains and then jump in.' Daisy pushed the duvet back and moved over to make room for him.

He snuggled up to her, and together they watched the dawn break over the upward sloping fields behind the bungalow, with hedges and trees casting long shadows.

'It's going to be a fine day, love,' she said as the sun rose, a brilliant orange-gold disc, into the clear blue sky.

'It's going to be a brill day!' Rupert exclaimed, wriggling with excitement.

Daisy laughed. 'You would say that if it was pouring with rain.'

Rupert giggled. 'I know,' he said. 'It would still be great if it was raining cats and dogs, as Aunt Mary used to say.'

'Do you still miss Aunt Mary?'

'Course I do, but the miss isn't so bad now, and I think she'd be pleased to know that we're living here, and you're the assistant matron and a VIP.'

'Hey, not so much of the VIP. I'm just a hard-working nurse.'

'I know, that's what Mr Hill says—that you're a great little worker and your heart's in the right place. He says that you and Dr Torrence make a good team, and Matron's lucky to have you both.'

At the mention of Adam's name, Daisy felt a thrill of

pleasure run through her. 'He didn't say that to you, did he?' That wasn't like the usually discreet Steven.

'Oh, of course not, Mum, he was talking to Mrs Hill, but I heard him.'

'Big ears,' said Daisy, ruffling his blond thatch of hair. 'Now off you go; you use the bathroom first while I get the breakfast started. We don't want to be late, do we?'

'No way. I hope Dr Torrence won't be late either.'

'I'm sure he won't be.'

'No, I don't think he will be—he's too nice,' said Rupert, with an innocent confidence in Adam that pleased Daisy enormously.

In fact Adam arrived well before the time they had arranged, and Rupert rushed to fling open the front door.

'Hello, Dr Torrence,' he greeted him eagerly. 'Brill, you're really early.'

'Of course I am; it's a special day,' said Adam seriously. 'Choosing a bike is an important business; we mustn't rush it.'

Daisy followed Rupert slowly down the hall from the kitchen, trying to quieten her fast-beating heart, feeling suddenly hesitant, almost shy, about seeing him. She wondered what he would say to her, how he would greet her. Would their meeting in front of Rupert be awkward? How could she let him know how she felt about him, explain why she had put the phone down on him the other night? In a fraction of a moment, her mind seethed with questions.

Their eyes met over her son's head. Adam gave her a long, searching look, then slowly a smile spread over his face as he read there what he wanted to see. It was as if he had spoken; it was as if he had said, I know you love me, and I love you. A gossamer thread seemed to draw them together. The air crackled between them, and for a moment Daisy felt that the two of them were alone together. It was magical, unreal.

The moment might have gone on forever, but deliberately she blinked to break the spell, and said in a near-normal voice, 'Good morning, Adam. Do come in. Would you like a coffee before we go?'

'Oh, Mum,' wailed Rupert. 'Do you have to have coffee? Can't we just go—please?' He turned a bright, pleading face from one to the other.

Adam gave Daisy a wry smile and raised his eyebrows. 'I think the answer to that is no,' he said quietly. His eyes glinted with a mixture of gentle humour and understanding as he looked down at Rupert then back at Daisy. 'We should be off as soon as possible. We'll have coffee in town, *after* we've bought the bike. I don't think your son can contain himself much longer, do you?'

Daisy gave a tremulous little laugh and shook her head. 'No, you're right. I think the sooner we're off the better. Rupert, love, fetch your anorak from your room, and my blue striped jacket and blue shoulder-bag from my wardrobe, and we'll be off.'

'OK.' He bolted from the sitting-room.

Adam stepped forward as soon as he was out of the door and, taking Daisy's unresisting hands in his, pulled her to him and kissed her gently on the mouth. He looked down into her upturned face and said softly, 'Daisy, tell me, before Rupert comes back, that I'm not mistaken, that you love me as much as I love you.'

'Yes,' she whispered, 'I love you, Adam.'

'Thank God for that,' he breathed. Swiftly he bent

and brushed her lips with his, then stepped away as Rupert burst back into the room.

Thrusting Daisy's coat and bag at her, he said eagerly, 'Come on, Mum, I'm ready.' He turned a beaming face to Adam. 'Can we go now, Dr Torrence, *please*?'

Adam smiled down at him and put a hand on his shoulder. 'Of course, old chap; let's be off. And, you know, I think you might call me Adam. After all, I've known you since you were a baby, and your mother and I are very old friends.'

Daisy's heart thumped with pleasure at Adam's suggestion and it filled her with happiness to see them standing side by side. Adam, handsome, tall, broad-shouldered, protective, looking down at blond, diminutive Rupert, with his happy, shining face, looking trustingly up at him. The two people she loved best. For the moment, everything in her world was in perfect harmony. This, she felt, would be a day to remember.

And that same feeling of perfection, of harmony, continued as the day wore on.

They were a long time in the cycle shop. Daisy had to admit that Rupert had been right about wanting a man around. It needed someone who knew about tyre pressure, brakes and gears to appreciate the subtleties of the myriad bikes on offer. Eventually a robust green and silver mountain bike was decided upon by the two of them, with Daisy having very little to do with the decision. But she came into her own when choosing a safety helmet.

Rupert fancied a flashy silver and green model that matched his bike, but she, backed up by Adam, insisted on a less colourful but more expensive red one that appeared to guarantee greater safety.

'Your mother's right, Rupert,' Adam said firmly. 'You must have only the best and safest in the way of protection. It makes good sense. And anyway, red will look great with your bike. Just the job.'

'Will it really—you're not just saying that to please Mum?'

'Certainly not. I've seen enough head injuries in my time to know the value of a good safety helmet.'

Rupert gave him a rather shy, trusting smile. 'OK, Dr Torrence—sorry, I mean Adam. I'll go along with the one that Mum's chosen, if you really think it's best.'

'Good lad,' said Adam. He and Daisy exchanged amused, intimate, loving smiles over Rupert's head as he bent over his new machine.

Daisy said softly, 'The Oracle has spoken, apparently. You can do no wrong.'

Adam raised one finely arched eyebrow and murmured, 'And long may it last. Let's hope it bodes well for the future—our future.'

He squeezed her hand gently as they stood side by side, looking down at Rupert's shining blond head. Daisy shivered at his touch, and a fresh wave of love for the large man and small child surged through her; sudden tears pricked at the back of her eyes.

'Hey, are you all right?' Adam asked, in a low, concerned voice.

Daisy smiled at him through a misty blur. 'Oh, I'm fine,' she murmured breathlessly. 'I'm so happy.'

And her happiness grew throughout the day, blossoming under Adam's admiring glances, or the occasional touch of his hand. Every look that he exchanged with her as they listened to Rupert's excited chatter said mutely, I love you.

And every little incident seemed special, like the way

she and Rupert giggled together at Adam's expression of mock-horror when he learned that they were lunching in a burger bar and not at the elegant French restaurant that he'd planned.

'I promised Rupert that he could choose where we had lunch,' said Daisy, eyes sparkling with fun as she looked up into Adam's rueful face. 'And he has chosen the burger bar, and it is, after all, his day.'

'True,' replied Adam, with a wry smile for Daisy. 'It's Rupert's day. Oh, lord, the perils of parenthood.' He gave her a conspiratorial wink and Rupert a gentle punch on the shoulder and pushed him ahead of them, across the busy pedestrian square. 'Go on, then, old chap; lead the way to this gourmet's delight that you're so keen on.'

Rupert frowned. 'Do you mean the burger bar?' he asked doubtfully.

'Indeed I do, if that's what tickles your palate.'

Rupert looked at him even more doutbfully. 'What do you mean, "tickles your palate"?'

Adam looked rather startled at being asked to explain himself. 'Well, I suppose it means having something that you fancy,' he said.

Rupert's face cleared. 'Oh, you mean, a little of what you fancy does you good, like Aunt Mary used to say.'

'Precisely.'

Grinning broadly, gently teasing Daisy, Rupert told him, 'Well, I fancy a burger and chips and all the things that Mum won't let me have at home.'

'Well, I suppose you'll survive all that saturated fat just this once,' said Adam, with a laugh, 'if your mum has no objection.'

Daisy shook her head and joined in the laughter, and was almost overwhelmed by a great surge of joy. She was elated; how wonderful it was for the three of them to fit together like a family. There was an easy rapport flowing between them. It wasn't her imagination. Already they seemed a unit, complete, as if they had covered in a few hours what might have taken years to achieve. It boded a bright and happy future, because if all was well between Adam and Rupert she was free to exult, without guilt or selfishness, in her love for this caring, sexy man.

She sighed with the sheer perfection of it all, and he caught her eye, and she knew that he understood what she had been thinking.

They were at one.

And this feeling of oneness continued in the cinema, where Daisy sat between Adam and Rupert to watch the delightful Disney film.

Occasionally, seemingly by accident, though she couldn't be sure of that, Adam would touch her hand or press his leg against hers and, like a young girl in love, she would tingle all over with pleasure. Once or twice, in the dim light of the auditorium, she glanced at his austere profile, and when he half turned to look at her she saw his mouth quirk at the corner and his eyes glint. Does he know the effect he is having on me? she wondered, and decided that he probably did, but that she really didn't mind. Why should she? To love and be loved was the ultimate happiness.

When they left the cinema, they sat in the courtyard garden of The Martletts, an old-fashioned tea parlour just off the square, and enjoyed home-made hot scones and jam, and honey and ginger cake.

Daisy and Adam could have sat there for hours in the late spring sunshine, just thrilled to be together, discussing the film they had just seen, television programmes they'd enjoyed, and a hundred other topics that interested them. But after a while Rupert, who had eaten a huge tea and happily joined in the conversation at times, began to grow restless.

'Mum,' he pleaded, 'do you think we can collect my bike from the shop soon, so that we can get home and I can try it out before dark?'

'Of course,' said Daisy, feeling a twinge of guilt, and at once contrite. 'You've been very patient, love.'

'You certainly have,' confirmed Adam, standing up immediately. 'So let's get going and fetch the precious bicycle and get back to Featherston as soon as possible.' He smiled down at Rupert and added, 'I'm really looking forward to seeing you go hell for leather round the green. I think I'll get my bike out and join you.'

Rupert beamed. 'Oh, will you? Wizard! Mega.'

A short while later, the bike, helmet, tool kit and panniers were safely stowed, under Rupert's anxious supervision, in the back of the Range Rover, then they drove out of Brighthelm and headed for home. At this time of the early evening the roads were fairly busy, but once they had left the outskirts of the town the traffic thinned out, and they bowled steadily east along the coast road towards the clinic, with the westering sun behind them.

They were all three silent with contentment, Rupert in seventh heaven because of his bike and Daisy and Adam in quiet contemplation of the love that seemed to have matured and blossomed between them throughout the day. The atmosphere in the car was euphoric.

They had travelled a few miles, each wrapped up in happy thoughts, when Adam, rousing himself from his reverie, thrilling to the presence of a radiantly warm, loving Daisy beside him and a happy Rupert in the back of the car, was suddenly mindful of his duties as host, and asked if either of them wanted the radio on.

'Oh, no,' Daisy said quickly in a low voice, 'not the radio; it would destroy. . .' she hesitated, afraid of sounding rather fanciful '. . .this special feeling.'

Adam gave her a quick sideways glance. 'I couldn't agree more,' he murmured.

They exchanged fleeting, understanding smiles.

'And I don't want to listen to the boring old radio either,' said Rupert, clearly bursting with energy and an excitement that he felt hard to contain. 'I want to *do* something. Why don't we have a sing-along like Mum and Aunt Mary and I used to have when we'd been on a shopping trip? That used to be brill, didn't it, Mum?'

'Brill,' confirmed Daisy. She was astonished and delighted and could have hugged him, knowing that he must be feeling relaxed and at ease with Adam to make such a suggestion. It was very much an intimate, family thing, shared previously only with herself and Aunt Mary, and, boy-like, Rupert was rather shy about singing in front of other people.

'Great idea,' said Adam in a pleased voice, obviously only too willing to go along with Rupert, perhaps even realising the significance of the suggestion coming from an eight-year-old boy. 'What shall we sing?'

'Do you know "Green Grow the Rushes O"? Mum does; we're learning it at school. Our music teacher says it's an old traditional song.'

Adam grinned. 'I know it,' he said. 'Learnt it when I was about your age. You start us off.'

'All right,' Rupert agreed. And, in a clear, tuneful treble, he began to sing, 'I'll give you One O, Green grow the Rushes O.'

'What is your One O?' chanted Daisy and Adam, she in a light soprano and he in a rich baritone.

'One is one and all alone and ever more shall be so,' trilled Rupert in reply.

And so they sang back and forth, in an elated, almost holiday mood as they cruised down the long, gentle slope of the cliff road towards the junction at the foot of the hill.

Daisy glanced round at Rupert's open, innocent face, and then sideways at Adam's strong, mature profile, and felt deeply and profoundly contented. The three of them singing joyfully, in harmony, together. It was a fitting ending to a perfect day. A foretaste of their future.

Smiling, she gazed ahead of her at the long, straight ribbon of the coastal road, undulating before them along the side of the downs. There wasn't much traffic about. A couple of cars coming towards them, and a truck coming down the steep lane from the village of Rushdean.

They would soon be home, and Rupert could try out his precious bike with Adam to accompany him. Wonderful. She would prepare supper for herself and Adam after Rupert had gone to bed and afterwards. . . Afterwards they would exchange loving, intimate gestures, and make plans for a shared and joyful future. Life was almost too good. She gave a great sigh of sheer happiness.

Glancing quickly at her, Adam took his hand from the wheel for a moment and patted her knee. 'Happy?'

'Totally.'

Rupert shrilled with great gusto, 'I'll give you Four O, Green grow the rushes O.'

And she and Adam responded with, 'What is your Four O?' as they reached the bottom of the hill.

Sunlight flashed on glass.

There was a sudden scream of brakes.

A dull thud.

Metal screeched on metal.

And then nothing.

Oblivion.

CHAPTER TEN

'DAISY . . . Daisy, love. . .wake up. . .come on, wake up.'

Muffled, blurred, from a long way off, the words penetrated Daisy's consciousness, but she couldn't open her eyes. Didn't want to open her eyes. Her lids felt like lead and her head ached. She'd had a dreadful sleep. Why did she have to wake up? Who was trying to make her wake up? She knew the voice, a deep, rich, warm sort of voice. Who? Who? She frowned, and frowning hurt. Her arm was trapped. She tried to move off her back, but moving hurt. Don't move! an inner voice warned her.

'Daisy, can you hear me? It's Adam.'

The voice again—nearer, clearer.

Adam! Adam! Of course Adam. Why was he calling her? Why did she feel so peculiar? Where was she—in her room? What was Adam doing in her room? She forced her eyes open and tried to focus them in the direction that the voice was coming from—but she couldn't turn her head. It was rigid, stiff; she could only swivel her eyes. She looked up at the ceiling. It was high, a long way off. Not her room.

Adam's face swam into view, looking down at her. He was coming closer. He looked odd, strange, different. Why did he have a patch over one eye and a line down his cheek? A line down his cheek, like a cut. . .a cut. . . How had he got a cut—and what had he done to his eye? She wanted to touch his cheek, but couldn't lift her hands.

Where was she? Why couldn't she move?

Hot tears of frustration pricked her eyes and spilled over. Adam wiped them away with a gentle finger. He bent over and brushed her lips with his. 'Welcome back,' he said softly.

She looked at him, scared. 'Help me,' she murmured, her breath coming in uneven, painful gasps as she spoke. 'I can't remember. Why can't I move? Where are we?'

'We're in Brighthelm General, my love, in Intensive Care.'

'Intensive Care...but why? Why?'

'We were involved in an accident.'

'An accident—what happened?'

'A heavy truck bashed into the side of us, coming out of Rushdean Lane. It's nearly midnight now. You've been unconscious for a few hours; that's why you can't remember clearly.'

'And why can't I move? Why does it hurt me to breathe?'

'You have a couple of cracked ribs, a badly bruised and lacerated shoulder and bruising to your left temple. You're wearing a support collar pro tem to keep your neck rigid and you're connected to a glucose and saline drip, though this will probably come out now you're conscious.' He deliberately spoke in a quiet, soothing, matter-of-fact voice to reassure her. 'Try not to panic, love, if you can't remember; it'll come back to you soon. Let it come gradually; don't force it.' He stroked a tendril of hair away from her cheek.

She winced as he touched a bruise, and stared up at

his own battered face. 'And you're hurt too, Adam,' she murmured. 'I'm so sorry.'

'But not badly,' he said. 'Don't worry about me. Only a few cuts and bruises and a minuscule piece of metal which has been removed from my eye. I've got to keep it covered for a couple of days, but it'll be fine.'

Don't worry, don't panic, he said, but that was just what she wanted to do: panic. Why couldn't she remember anything? Why was everything a blank, like a big black hole? There was something important she wanted to ask, needed to know, had to worry about, but she couldn't think what it was. She was *so* tired. She was glad that Adam was here, sitting beside her bed. He would take care of everything. Her hand in his, she closed her eyes and half slept.

She was aware of movement and voices round her bed, turning her, rearranging her pillows, taking off the neck collar, removing the drip. But she lay still and kept her eyes closed.

There was something that she had to remember, must remember. She must try to concentrate. Something, something. . .

Half conscious, memory began to ooze back sluggishly. Adam said there had been an accident. Dimly she recalled a bang, noise, screeching. But there was something important before that that she must remember. . . What was it? That's right; they were singing, the three of them were singing. . .'Green grow. . .' Rupert was—

Rupert! His name came out like a scream in her head, but her lips wouldn't frame the letters.

Why hadn't she remembered Rupert before? How could she have forgotten him? Why hadn't Adam said anything about him? What was he keeping from her?

Terror flooded through her. She struggled to sit up, ignoring the pain in her side and shoulder. Where is Rupert? she cried silently. Oh, my darling boy, where are you? She was afraid to ask. But had to ask. She had to know.

'Rupert,' she gasped, her voice high-pitched, cracked, croaking. 'Is he—is he all right? Please tell me. *Tell me.*' She clutched at Adam's arm. Dread filled her. 'Is he—is he. . .?' Her eyes held the question that she couldn't utter.

Adam pushed her gently back on to the pillow, and held her trembling hands in both of his. 'No,' he said firmly, knowing exactly what she had meant, had feared to ask, 'he's not dead. He's unconscious, but he's alive, though he's been injured. He's in Theatre at the moment having surgery.'

'Surgery! Emergency surgery? Is he in danger? How badly has he been hurt? Is it a head injury, internal injuries? Tell me, Adam, tell me everything. What's wrong? What's happened to him? I have to know.' The words tumbled out in an incoherent, painful rush as she tried to speak and breathe. Her eyes pleaded with him.

Adam kept her hands clasped firmly in his, willing her to be brave, trying to let her know that he was there for her, offering her his strength, quelling his own fears for Rupert. He mustn't be too emotional; it wouldn't help her.

Keeping his voice flat and informative, almost as if he were lecturing a classful of students, he said, 'He had a pretty bad blow on the head, but he's had an X-ray and been seen by a neurologist and there's no fracture or brain damage. . .'

'Oh, thank God for that—thank God,' she whispered.

'But he's got internal injuries, Daisy; they don't know yet how severe. There's a possibility that his spleen might be ruptured.'

'But they can deal with that, can't they? Even if they have to remove it, he could cope, couldn't he, Adam? I've nursed patients who. . .' She faltered to a stop, and tried desperately to calm herself. She must try to get a grip on herself, but how could she? For this wasn't a patient, this was her son she was talking about, her precious son. However hard she tried, she couldn't be professional, detached.

Adam looked down into her anguished eyes as she silently begged him to reassure her. And yet she wanted the truth, and he knew that he had to tell it to her.

He *wanted* to take her in his arms and hold her tight and tell her that there was nothing to worry about. He *wanted* to take the pain and distress out of her eyes by watering down the truth. But he resisted. He sensed that side-stepping the issue wouldn't help her. She wanted hard, professional facts.

He said, again in his impersonal, lecturing voice, 'Yes, he would be able to manage quite well without his spleen. *If* they do a splenectomy, he'll be immunised with pneumococcal vaccine and given long-term antibiotics to guard against infection. That's the drill with children. It's possible even to implant a piece of undamaged spleen which might regenerate to form a new, healthy organ.'

'Do you think that's what they're doing now in Theatre—a splenectomy?' she asked, her voice trembling as she took another painful breath.

'I don't know, love. They suspect that he's haemorrhaging, but it might not be a severe bleed. It's impossible to tell from the X-rays, so they're having a look to see what damage has been done.' He gave her hand a squeeze and leaned over, kissing her cheek with infinite tenderness. 'But there is something else,' he said slowly, dreading what he had to tell her. 'It's Rupert's legs, Daisy. They've been badly damaged, particularly his left leg and foot. They took the full brunt of the impact when the truck struck us.'

'What are you saying, Adam?' Fear, like an icy hand, gripped her heart. Ragged breathing tore at her side.

'That he has multiple fractures, and nerve and muscle damage. But Joe Field, the top orthopaedic surgeon, is going to operate as soon as Rupert's internal injuries have been made safe. He will certainly immobilise his legs and do any emergency work. But it's imperative that full surgery's performed as soon as possible, in order to. . .'

'To save his foot and leg.' Daisy finished the sentence for him in a whisper. Numb with shock at the possibility that Rupert might have to have an amputation, she let silent tears run down her face.

Adam bent and kissed her wet cheeks. 'Joe Field's a brilliant surgeon,' he said softly. 'If anyone can save Rupert's leg, he can.'

Early on Sunday morning, while Rupert was still in the recovery unit following his ordeal in Theatre, Daisy was moved out of Intensive Care into a side-room on the same floor.

Because of her cracked ribs she was still in excruciating pain on breathing. Her whole body was stiff and bruised, but she wasn't in danger and her anxiety for Rupert made her virtually indifferent to her own pain.

A short while after she'd been moved, Philip Green, the general surgeon, and Joe Field, the orthopod, came to her straight from the theatre to report on Rupert's progress. Numb with apprehension, Daisy learned that there hadn't been any need to perform an amputation or a splenectomy. They had been able to stem the bleeding in his abdomen by doing minor repairs to blood vessels, which should heal quickly, and Mr Field professed himself, cautiously, pleased with the job he'd done on Rupert's legs, though he thought he might have to operate on his left leg again at some future date, depending on how it healed. But his leg and foot were going to be saved.

Almost overwhelmed with relief, making a valiant effort to rein in her emotions, Daisy thanked the surgeons, but when they had gone she gave way to a storm of weeping in Adam's comforting arms.

Now all she wanted to do was to see Rupert—touch him, let him know that she was there, that he was not alone. And some time after he was moved to Intensive Care she was told that she might pay him a brief visit.

She was too shaky to walk so Adam, who had remained with her, took her in a wheelchair to his bedside.

With difficulty she held back her tears as she gazed at her son lying in the hospital bed attached to a forest of wires, drips and machinery. He looked small, pinched, pale and vulnerable. The left side of his face and head was bruised and swollen. A cradle lifted the bedclothes off his legs. But she was assured by the unit sister that he was deeply and naturally asleep after coming round from the anaesthetic.

Daisy took his tiny, limp hand in hers and held it tightly. 'I'm here, darling,' she murmured through stiff lips. 'Mummy's here.'

He didn't stir. Long, gold-tipped lashes curled against pallid cheeks.

Adam said quietly, after glancing at the monitor, 'His readings are good. He's doing fine, Daisy, as well as can be expected. He's got everything going for him; he's a tough little chap, a real fighter.'

'Yes, he always has been,' she whispered. 'He got over all his childhood ailments without any problems, but I wish he would speak to me; I wish he knew that I was here.'

'He will next time you see him. I bet he'll be bright as a button; you know what kids are. But we should let him sleep now. It's the best medicine of all. Sister will let us know when he wakes up, and we can be back here in a few minutes and then you can talk to him.'

But Adam had left to return to Featherston Hall before Rupert woke from his first long sleep early on Sunday evening, and Daisy was assisted to his bedside by a nurse.

He looked at her with blurry eyes, and for one horrified moment she thought that he didn't recognise her. But he did. His eyes cleared. 'Mum,' he whispered, 'it's you; I'm glad.' And to her delight and amazement, ill as he was, a ghost of a smile hovered round his soft pink mouth.

Ignoring the pain in her ribs, she leaned over, kissed him and smoothed a thick lock of hair back from his forehead. 'How do you feel, love?'

'I feel sort of sore here——' he pointed to the left side of his abdomen '—and my legs hurt; they feel funny and stiff. The doctors and nurses said that I was in an accident, but I don't remember it. Was I badly hurt?'

Daisy took a deep breath; now was the moment of truth.

Both Joe Field and Philip Green had advised her to put him in the picture, if he asked what had happened. 'Children are remarkably tough and resilient and can take the truth,' they'd said. 'But give him the good news first. Explain that the operation that we had to do on his tummy was a success, and he's already on the mend. And when you tell him that his legs have been injured stress the fact that his right leg wasn't too badly hurt and needed only minor repairs.

'Then break it to him gently that his left leg may need more attention to get it back to normal. Let him know that he'll soon be mobile, though he might have to wear caliper splints for a while. From what Adam's said, he's an intelligent lad; be honest wtih him. You're his mum, and he'll appreciate you being straight with him rather than trying to prevaricate.'

They had made it sound almost easy, but now, looking at Rupert lying in bed, a small boy, wide-eyed and vulnerable, she wondered if they had been right. How could she tell him that he might have to have another operation on his leg at some later date, perhaps more than one?

She longed for Adam's comforting presence. He would have known what to do, what to say, how to say it.

Adam! Even the thought of him gave her a spurt of courage and confidence and, picking her words with great care, she found herself telling Rupert everything about the accident and about his condition, just as she had been advised.

She hadn't really known what to expect, but the surgeons had been right. Rupert took what she had to say with astonishing calmness. And, considering that he had just wakened from a long, deep, post-anaesthetic sleep, he seemed surprisingly bright and alert. He listened thoughtfully to what she had to say, and asked several intelligent questions to which she tried to give honest answers.

'Will I be able to walk again properly?' he wanted to know. 'Without this caliper thing.'

'Yes, love. Mr Field, the orthopaedic surgeon, is pretty confident that you will eventually, but it will take some time.'

'Will I be able to ride my bike?' he asked.

The unexpected question nearly floored her. It seemed incredible that he should be thinking of the bike at a time like this. A bitter thought crossed her mind. If it hadn't been for the wretched bike, they would never have been travelling along the coast road in the Range Rover and the accident would never have happened.

She put the thought behind her and said cheerfully, 'Yes, of course you will. But we'll have to get a new one—the one we bought on Saturday was completely smashed up, I'm afraid.'

'Golly, that truck must have been big and hit us hard to bash up a Range Rover—they're pretty tough. I bet Adam was mad about it; it was almost new.' He frowned, staring at her with wide, anxious eyes, and asked in a small, shaky voice, 'I say, Mum, where is Adam? Was he hurt in the crash? And were you hurt? You look all right, but were you?' Suddenly fearful, he clutched at her arm.

'We were both injured, love,' she said quietly. 'But not too seriously. In fact, Adam is well enough to start work, and has gone back to Featherston. But I'm staying here at the hospital for a few days to be near you.'

'Oh, great,' he said feelingly. 'So we're all all right. Mega.' His eyelids drooped. 'Gosh, I'm tired,' he murmured, and, closing his eyes, fell suddenly asleep.

Adam, minus the eye patch, and with a narrow strip of plaster covering the cut on his cheek, returned Monday evening. He looked professional and elegant in a charcoal-grey suit, pristine white shirt and restrained striped tie, every inch the senior medical man that he was.

Daisy, who had spent most of the day in Intensive Care with a steadily improving Rupert, was resting on her bed, propped up against a mound of pillows, when he arrived. Somewhat comforted and more relaxed on account of Rupert's improvement, she had been letting her thoughts drift back over the events of the last forty-eight hours.

What an absolute tower of strength Adam had been. He had taken care of everything Saturday evening, while she'd been unconscious. He had spoken with Matron Browning and put her in the picture. He had even thought to phone Janice Hill and ask her to bring in some clothes for herself and Rupert, which, making a flying visit, she had managed to deliver on Sunday morning. And he had made statements to the police about the accident. He had stayed with Rupert until he went into Theatre and had then returned to sit by her bedside until she recovered consciousness.

What would she have done without him? She ached to see him, longed to share her hopes and fears for Rupert with him. She needed him desperately, needed his commanding presence, his compassionate love.

And quite suddenly there he was, arms full of flowers, watching her from the doorway. Her heart rocketed at the sight of him, and a great wave of relief surged through her. He was here; all would be well. He would be with her to support and reassure her. 'Oh, Adam, you've come,' she blurted out breathlessly, as if he were the last person in the world she had expected to see.

'As promised,' he said softly, and his firm mouth curved into a warm, tender, intimate smile. He crossed the room and stood looking down at her. His dark, piercing gaze searched her face intently, clinically, accurately reading the signs of sleeplessness and pain in the smudges beneath her eyes and the droop of her wide mouth. 'You look tired, my darling,' he remarked in his deep, rich voice, seeming to invest the words with a special significance. 'How are you feeling today?'

His darling! 'Fine, much better,' she said, smiling up at him, ignoring the dull ache in her side. And a thousand times better now that you're here, she wanted to add, but she didn't, for suddenly she felt unaccountably shy.

He bent to kiss her, his cool lips lingering on hers, and then trailing with butterfly gentleness across her bruised temple beneath her golden fringe of hair. She was conscious of the smoothness of his cologne-scented skin before he drew slowly, reluctantly away. He must have just shaved. When she'd last seen him, he'd had a thick growth of stubble on his strong jaw, which, together with the patch over his eye, had made him look like a swashbuckling pirate.

He pulled a chair up to the side of her bed, lowered himself into it, and took her hand in his. 'Now tell me all about Rupert,' he said. 'How's our young chap doing?'

It was wonderfully comforting to have her hand in his

and to have him ask about Rupert as if he really cared. She breathed in hard, and tried to stifle her subsequent gasp as pain stabbed at her cracked ribs.

'He's improving rapidly. I can hardly believe it. They tell me that it won't be long before he's moved into the children's ward. He's incredibly cheerful in spite of knowing that he might have to have another op on his left leg and foot eventually. Oh, Adam, he's so little and yet so brave, it doesn't seem possible. He's taken all that I and the doctors told him about his condition almost without turning a hair. Do you know, he even asked yesterday about his bike?'

'His precious bike. Does he know that it was smashed up?'

'Yes, I told him, but I said that I'd get him another.'

'*We'll* get him another, Daisy, you and I.'

'But, Adam, I can't let you——'

'No buts, love,' he interrupted firmly. 'It's not a question of letting me. When the times comes for him to have another bike, we'll be married and I shall be *in loco parentis*—I'll be entitled to buy him expensive presents.'

She gaped at him, and took in a rasping breath. For a moment, she couldn't speak. 'M-married! Adam, whatever do you mean? What are you saying?' she asked at last in an unsteady voice.

He said simply, his voice cool, detached almost, 'I'm saying that I want to marry you, Daisy, and the sooner the better. What's the point in waiting? We belong together; we both know it. And you need me now, not at some vague future date. I've never felt so certain of anything in my life. I told you the other day that I love you and want to take care of you for always. Nothing's changed. I feel the same now as I did then, in fact even more strongly since the accident. You must believe me; I'm not given to making promises that I don't keep.'

His eyes, dark, enigmatic pools, met hers steadily.

'Oh, Adam,' she whispered, 'of course I believe you. But we need time to get to know each other again. This is too quick, too sudden.'

Adam shook his head. 'Not true,' he said brusquely. 'We don't need time. We already know all there is to know about each other. We've wasted enough time being apart; don't let's waste any more. We were drawn towards each other all those years ago, but we were blind then, when we were young, I more blind than you.'

'Blind?' Daisy stared at him, her violet-blue eyes puzzled. 'I don't understand.'

'Blind to the fact that you were only infatuated with Matthew, nothing more. You were never in love with him. You were drawn to me, but resisted, remember? And I was madly and utterly in love with you, Daisy, but gave you up because I thought that you and Matthew had a serious thing going. He was my best friend, and you were the only girl for me. In my youthful innocence I decided that I would be noble. I couldn't muck up your lives, so I made myself scarce— went abroad with the VSO, and later to Africa. Stayed out of the way most of the time.'

The truth suddenly hit her. 'Adam, are you saying that I'm your long-lost love?' she asked slowly, incredulously. 'The one you told me about?'

'Yes.' He stood up, leaned over the bed and cradled her face in his hands, his thumbs gently stroking her cheeks. 'You were my long-lost love, and I sure as hell don't mean to lose you again. You've admitted that you love me, need me, Daisy. There's nothing to stop us getting married, is there?'

Her heartbeats quickened, and she felt, as she had once before, that she was drowning in his dark, liquid brown eyes full of intense passion. And she *wanted* to drown in his eyes, to feel his arms round her, strong, comforting and safe, and yet so exciting. She longed to say, No, there's nothing to stop us getting married, but knew that she couldn't. If only she could! But there was another love in her life. A young, vulnerable, dependent love. 'There's Rupert,' she whispered.

Adam went very still; his thumbs stopped caressing her cheeks though his eyes remained fixed on hers. He said in a low voice, 'Rupert? But I want to care for him as I care for you. I love him because I love you and because I loved Matthew. I don't see that there's a problem.'

Daisy said carefully, afraid of hurting his feelings, searching for the right words, yet knowing that she must be honest with him, 'Adam, there might or might not be a problem; I don't know. It depends on Rupert. Children are unpredictable. He doesn't know about us, not about the way we feel about each other. All he knows is that we're old friends. We've hardly had time to come to terms with our present feelings ourselves— at least I haven't.

'But if it hadn't been for the accident I would have told him how we feel about each other by now.

'He likes and admires you, but he may not want to share me with you permanently, on a full-time basis. He's been used to having me to himself. And now, with the accident and the prospect of being at least temporarily disabled, he's going to need me more than ever.'

'I rather thought he'd need us both,' said Adam, with

a wry smile, as he slowly dropped his hands from her face. 'And I thought that *you* needed me.' He kissed her gently and straightened up. 'It seems I was wrong.'

She was shocked. 'Oh, no, Adam, not wrong; please don't think that. I need your friendship, your love desperately, but I don't know, after all that's happened, if I can marry you. I can't commit myself, not yet anyway. It wouldn't be fair to you or to Rupert. Please understand. Don't be angry.'

Adam shook his head. His long, lean face looked, all at once, tired and very gaunt. 'Oh, I'm not angry, love,' he said gently. 'Just disappointed. I happen to believe that your reasons are wrong for being reluctant to make a commitment. You underestimate the rapport that exists between Rupert and me. Given the chance, I think he would welcome me into the family. But you must give him the opportunity to say so by being honest with him, just as you have been about his physical condition. Children are tough. Don't over-protect him, Daisy. Don't let *your* pride, and the fact that you've managed as a single parent over the years, create problems where none exists. Let me into your life to help. Don't make mountains out of molehills.'

What did he mean, mountains out of molehills? Rupert's happiness wasn't a molehill. Why wouldn't he understand? Tears stung her eyes. Suddenly she felt unutterably weary. She couldn't talk any more, not even to Adam. She wanted to be alone with her thoughts.

Perceptive as ever, Adam said softly, 'But you're tired, love; we've talked enough. I'm sorry if I've exhausted you.' He brushed a kiss across her wide, lovely, drooping mouth. 'We'll talk some more, some other time, when you're stronger. Get things sorted out. Goodnight, dear girl, sleep well.' Abruptly he crossed the room and blew her a kiss as he reached the door before disappearing into the corridor.

She marshalled her muddled thoughts when he had gone and mulled over what he had said. What had he meant about pride creating problems? He seemed to have inferred that she would let pride, and not concern for Rupert, prevent her from marrying him. As if she would! But could he have meant that? Could he so have misunderstood her? All she wanted was happiness for the three of them; surely he could see that? Was he right in suggesting that she ask Rupert how he felt? Was she being cowardly not to do so? Would it be fair to Rupert, who, although he was improving at an astonishing rate, was still an ill child?

There was knock at the door, and the night nurse came in offering a milky drink, analgesics, and the latest gossip. Daisy was grateful for the interruption to her jumbled, unhappy thoughts, and when the nurse had gone, too tired to think any more, she found herself drifting off into a dreamless sleep.

The following morning, Tuesday, brought get-well cards for her and Rupert from the staff and children at Featherston, and from the village school. And there was a long, reassuring letter from Matron Browning addressed to Daisy, wishing both her and Rupert well, and hoping that they were making good progress. She wrote:

> And don't worry about your future here at the clinic; we will work something out about how you can look after Rupert and carry on with your work until

he's fit enough to return to school. Everyone is anxious to help. Just get well and come home soon.
Bless you both,
Helen.

'Home'. What a lovely word. A warm glow spread through Daisy. Trust Helen Browning to find the right thing to say. A kind and generous woman, she had, with practical sympathy, let Daisy know that her job at Featherston was safe, even though she hadn't quite completed her probationary period.

She gave a great sigh of relief. A secure future was one thing she didn't have to worry about. She had a job and a home, and could concentrate on getting Rupert through the next weeks and months with plenty of support from Matron and the other staff.

And, of course, she had Adam. Her heartbeat quickened as her thoughts turned back to the conversation of the night before and his offer of marriage. Without a shred of doubt she knew that he would always support her, whatever her decision was about marrying him. He might be hurt and bitterly disappointed if she refused him, but he had made it clear that he would never stop loving her. He had loved her too long.

Was he right about telling Rupert how they felt about each other and getting his reaction? Was she being over-protective? Or was she feeling vulnerable on her own account? Could she possibly be afraid of sharing Rupert's care and affection with anyone else, even the man she loved? Or was she too proud to accept such help?

More endless, unanswerable questions. Perhaps time

or inspiration would give her some answers. She would have to play the situation by ear and act on intuition.

She gathered up the letters and cards that had arrived that morning and made her way slowly and thoughtfully to Rupert in Intensive Care.

'Hi, Mum,' he greeted her happily. 'I'm going to be moved into the children's ward today as I'm doing so well. Isn't that mega? There'll be other kids to talk to and television to watch.'

'Oh, Rupert, love, that's really wonderful,' said Daisy, with a wide smile, bending to kiss his flushed cheek. A tide of gratitude and relief swept over her as she realised that, for the moment at least, he was out of danger and on the road to recovery. 'A great step forward. I am pleased.'

'And I can have more visitors there. I bet Tom will come to see me, and Mr and Mrs Hill, and some of my other friends. And perhaps even Adam might come, if he's not too busy. That would be brill, mega,' he added eagerly, using his favourite word of praise to descibe his feelings.

Daisy's heart lurched. Adam had been right about the extra-special rapport that had arisen between him and Rupert in such a short while. Rupert's eyes had brightened when he'd spoken of him, and he had mentioned Adam several times over the last couple of days, wanting to know how he was and when he would see him. Could he be missing him? Was it a sign that she should tell him about Adam's proposal of marriage? Would it please him to know that Adam wanted to be a father to him? But she knew that no way could she decide now—she needed to think about it a bit more.

She said softly, 'Of course he'll be visiting you, love, as soon as possible. He came to see me last night, and would have called to see you then, but you were fast asleep.'

'Well, I won't be asleep next time he comes 'cos I'm not feeling so tired now. He can tell me all about the crash, and we can talk about the new bike that I'm going to have. Do you think he'll help me choose it like he did the last one?'

'Yes, I'm sure he will. But, Rupert, do you really want to know about the crash?'

'Course I do. And everyone at school will want to know about it.'

'Oh, I see,' she said lamely. But she didn't really. Was this the divide between a one- and two-parent family? she wondered. Was male and female thinking so different on some things? Did boys *need* a male role model? Did they always want to know all the gory details about everything?

For once she felt really out of tune with Rupert and was glad when a porter and a nurse arrived to move him to the paediatric unit, interrupting their conversation.

CHAPTER ELEVEN

ONCE transferred, Rupert settled down immediately in the free-and-easy atmosphere of the brightly decorated children's ward. In no time at all he was chattering away happily to several other young patients who had clustered round his bed, eager to talk to a new arrival.

Watching his animated face as he chatted with the other children, Daisy felt that, for the first time since Sunday, he didn't need her undivided attention. She sat back in her chair and, only half listening to the babble of talk going on around her, let her thoughts drift back to yesterday evening and her conversation with Adam.

He had been bitterly disappointed and, though he had denied it, a little angry that she would not tell Rupert that he wanted to marry her. 'You underestimate the rapport that exists between Rupert and me,' he'd said. 'Given the chance, I think he would welcome me into the family. But you must give him the opportunity to say so. . .'

Could he be right? He'd been so sure that Rupert would take the news in his stride and not be upset by it, even if he was not immediately in favour of them marrying. 'Children are tough,' he'd said, repeating what the surgeons had said when advising her to be honest about Rupert's physical condition. 'Don't overprotect him.'

So why was she reluctant to tell Rupert of Adam's proposal? Was it pride, or some primitive maternal instinct that selfishly made her unwilling to share the care of him with anybody, as Adam had hinted?

No! Fiercely she rejected the idea. The sole reason for her reluctance to break the news to Rupert was concern for him and Adam, nothing else. The thought of the three of them living together as a family filled her with a glow of warmth and happiness. It was what she wanted more than anything else in the world.

And she longed for and needed Adam's physical love, needed his authoritative, dominant masculinity after years of being without a man in her life. They had had few opportunities to express their feelings, but their brief encounters over the last few weeks had roused the sexuality that she had been suppressing for years.

She *wanted* to give herself to him wholly and completely; both physically and emotionally. She *wanted* him to take her in his arms and make passionate love to her. She *wanted* to be married to him. The very thought of his maleness, the smell and feel of him, thrilled her to the core.

But she knew that whatever her feelings, her needs, her wants she had to be cautious, keep a cool head, and face up to facts. She'd had one disastrous marriage, ultimately having to decide between her husband and her son's safety, and she wouldn't risk marrying again and jeopardising the happiness of herself, Rupert and Adam.

Of course, Adam was a stable and responsible man, unlike Matthew, and there would never be a repeat of the circumstances that had broken up her first marriage. But every marriage had its problems at times and needed to be worked at. Adam would make a fine and loving stepfather, but there would perhaps be times when he and Rupert might be at odds, as could happen in any father-son relationship, and she might have to arbitrate.

She had to be sure that her love was strong enough to withstand that sort of strain, and that she was capable of sharing her love evenly between them at all times. Neither Adam nor Rupert must ever feel that she was short-changing him.

A sudden wave of optimism washed over her. She *was* quite sure that she had an abundance of love for both of them. What she had to do now was to find out what Rupert's feelings were on the matter. That was the crucial factor.

Resolutely she made up her mind. Adam was right; there was no point in holding back. As soon as the opportunity presented itself she would put Rupert in the picture and he could say his piece. He could tell her honestly if he wanted Adam as a stepfather, or if he wanted their present relationship to continue unchanged, temporarily or permanently. She would be guided by his reaction to what she had to tell him. Their future happiness would be in his small hands, though he must never know it.

She wouldn't pressure him to make a decision, or try to influence him, though she would be honest with him about how she felt about Adam, if he wanted to know.

The noisy arrival of the dinner trolley intruded on her thoughts, and the children gathered round Rupert drifted away to sit at the table set up in the ward. Only Rupert remained in bed, immobilised because of his legs; he enjoyed a light meal of soup followed by ice-cream, and Daisy, knowing that on his own he needed her again, sat with him and chatted while he ate.

The children were encouraged to rest for an hour after their main meal, and, leaving Rupert dozing,

Daisy made her way to her room to have her own lunch and then take a rest herself.

She was making good progress following the accident, but found that she tired easily, and was still stiff and sore. But in spite of her various aches and pains, with Rupert now happily settled in the paediatric unit, she planned to return to Featherston shortly. She couldn't remain idle; she owed it to Matron Browning to start work as soon as possible. She would make arrangements to go home within the next few days.

Propped up against a mound of pillows, relaxed and almost asleep, she sensed rather than heard that somebody was in the room. Opening sleep-heavy lids, she found Adam standing beside her, looking down at her with his dark, luminous, enigmatic eyes, a half-smile on his lips. *Déjà vu*. It was almost a repeat of his appearance yesterday, when his silent arrival had surprised her. For such a large man, he moved remarkably quietly.

Her rhythmic heartbeat quickened. Her breath came in short, painful gasps, thumping against her cracked ribs. It was so good to see him. She thought he was looking even more ruggedly handsome than ever, in spite of the fading bruise shadowing the long cut on his lean cheek. The sight of him sent a thrill of pleasure trickling through her. This was the man who had secretly loved her for years. She was his long-lost love!

'Adam!' She held out both her hands.

He took them in his and, raising them to his lips, turned them over, kissing the palms gently, almost reverently, somehow making it seem the most natural thing in the world, and not in the least pretentious. 'Are you pleased to see me, Daisy?' he asked.

'You know I am,' she said breathlessly, smiling up at him, her violet-blue eyes revealing her love.

He perched himself on the side of her bed so that his face was almost level with hers. 'That's good,' he said softly, with a wry smile. 'So you're not angry with me for speaking my mind yesterday?'

Daisy shook her head. 'Oh, no; in fact I thought you might be angry with me for prevaricating over telling Rupert about us.'

'Well, I'm not, my love; be assured of that. I appreciate how you felt. It must have seemed that I was pressuring you, although that was the last thing that I meant to do—and you were so tired, it was thoughtless of me.' He put a finger under her chin, tilted her head and examined her face closely, his eyes dark and intense. He nodded, as if he approved of what he saw. 'But you look better today—more relaxed, less weary.'

'Oh, I'm over the moon, tons better, because Rupert was moved to the children's ward this morning. Isn't that super? He's so much improved, Adam, it's unbelievable. All in such a short while. Of course, he's still being given analgesics for the pain in his legs, and antibiotics against infection. But he's bright and cheerful, and chatting with the other children. It's hard to believe that he's been through such trauma over the last few days.'

Adam smiled broadly. 'That's absolutely great news—mega, as Rupert would say.' He leaned forward and gave her a warm, lingering but gentle kiss, restraining himself, as if he sensed that she couldn't cope with anything more passionate at that moment. 'He's obviously making tremendous progress. I'm looking forward to seeing him this afternoon.'

'And he's longing to see you. He said so this morning. He's missed you, Adam; he made that quite plain.'

Adam looked pleased, almost smug. 'Did he really? Well, I shouldn't be surprised. I *know* that he and I have something special going for us,' he said firmly, taking her hands in his and pressing them hard. 'It's difficult to explain, but I feel so close to him, Daisy, and I'm sure he senses it too. Why don't you take your courage in both hands and tell him about us? He's well enough now to be told; don't you agree?'

'Yes, I do, and I made up my mind just this morning to do so. But in my own time, over the next few days. I must choose the moment. It'll be a shock to him, whatever his feelings are. There'll be a lot for him to come to terms with. And supposing. . .'

'Supposing?'

She put a tentative hand on his arm. 'Supposing he doesn't want me to marry you, doesn't want you as a stepfather. . .' Her voice trailed away.

'Face that hurdle when it comes. *If* it comes,' he said, adding confidently, 'But I don't believe he will reject me, since we have this natural affinity with each other.'

'But, Adam, he's known you for such a short while. He has nothing from the past to remember you by. You're just his father's friend who has recently come into his life.'

'True, though time doesn't mean much to children, and instinct is a strange phenomenon. Don't rule it out. Perhaps he's drawn to me because he senses how close you and I and Matthew were. And he's seen photographs of Matthew, and there are physical similarities; perhaps that's influenced him. Maybe he's already cast me in the role of the father he can't remember.'

'Do you think that's possible?'

'Anything's possible. Who knows how his young mind and emotions are working? All I know is that the vibes between us are extraordinarily strong, and have been since we first met.' His voice dropped to a deep, husky drawl. 'But that's not surprising, considering how I feel about you, my dear, darling, lovely Daisy. He is, after all, your son. Your flesh and blood.'

Abruptly he stood up, took her hands in his and eased her off the bed, pulling her to him and folding her into his arms in one swift movement. He stared at her pale, upturned face framed by the bob of daffodil-yellow hair. 'You're like a flower, all white and gold,' he murmured. 'Such a delicate face, such lovely eyes.'

His own eyes were dark, fathomless pools of passion. He dropped feather-light, butterfly kisses on her cheeks, nose and eyelids, and finally on her mouth. She trembled as his tongue teased at her lips, parting them, briefly exploring the moist interior. But after a moment he lifted his head and groaned. 'Oh, Daisy,' he said, with a wry grin, 'again it's the wrong time and place for making love, but one day we'll get it right and make up for lost time.' With a long forefinger he traced the line of her small firm chin and slender throat.

Ignoring her bruised shoulder and cracked ribs, she twined her arms round his neck and pushed her fingers through his short, thick hair. 'Oh, Adam, I love you so much,' she murmured against his mouth.

'And I you, with all my heart,' he said fervently, planting a firm kiss on her parted lips. And then, gently untwining her arms, he eased her from him and told her softly, 'But that's enough for now, love; time we went to see that boy of ours.'

* * *

Rupert's face lit up when he saw Adam. 'Hi,' he said. 'Mum told me you would come if you had time.'

'I made time,' said Adam, 'especially to see you. It's nice to find you awake. The last time I was here you were snoring, and well and truly out for the count.' He ruffled Rupert's hair and they grinned at each other as if at some private joke.

'I don't snore,' Rupert asserted. 'Only old people snore.'

'Don't you believe it,' laughed Adam. 'Take my word for it, you can snore at any age—like this.' He snorted loudly and Rupert giggled.

Daisy watched and listened, glowing with happiness as they talked together, marvelling at the way they responded so naturally to each other. There was no doubt that they were on the same wavelength. Surely it was a good omen? Adam was right; they certainly had something special between them. They seemed even closer than some natural fathers and sons. Everything indicated that Rupert would welcome having Adam as a father, and her fears that he would turn down the suggestion when she put it to him now seemed groundless.

So why did she feel uneasy when it looked as if her dearest wish was to be realised? A little shaft of doubt, of guilt niggled as a thought struck her. Adam! Was she being fair to him by giving in to his desire to marry her immediately? Shouldn't she insist that they wait a bit, not rush things, give themselves more time to think things through? He'd seemed so sure of himself when he'd proposed that they marry as soon as possible, but had he felt pushed by the accident and her need for support? In normal circumstances, wouldn't he have taken his time before committing himself irrevocably?

It was all right from her point of view. Marriage to Adam would resolve all her problems. She would have his constant help and love, and no longer have to cope as a single parent. But what would he get out of it? Very little, she thought sadly as a sudden wave of pessimism engulfed her. He would get the woman whom he had professed to love for many years, and a perhaps partially disabled stepson! And that was it. Big deal. It didn't seem a very equitable return for what he would be giving to her and Rupert.

Supposing at some future date he resented the fact that they were dependent on him? It could happen, even to someone as balanced and logical and loving as Adam, even in the best of relationships.

It was a frightening scenario, love turned sour.

Her insides knotted up at the thought.

She became aware that she had been frowning down at her lap, and that Adam was watching her. She looked up and met his eyes across the bed, over Rupert's bent head. For the moment the boy was engrossed in the electronic pocket game that Adam had brought him and was oblivious of them both.

Adam said softly, with a faint smile, 'A penny for them.'

'What?' she asked.

'Your thoughts.'

'Oh, they were just daydreams,' she said dismissively.

'Worrying daydreams? You were frowning.' Eyebrows raised, he looked at her questioningly.

She knew then that she couldn't keep her unquiet thoughts to herself. He had to know what she was thinking. She had to explain herself to him, make him listen. 'I. . . I. . . We must talk, Adam,' she said in an urgent whisper, glancing at Rupert, who was still absorbed in his game.

Adam nodded. 'All right.' He looked at his wristwatch and touched Rupert's shoulder. 'I'll have to be off now, old chap. And if you don't mind I'm going to steal your mother away to walk me to my car and get a breath of air. I think she needs it, OK?'

Rupert looked up from his game. 'OK. Will you come again tomorrow?' he asked. 'Please,' he entreated, his big brown eyes pleading.

'Of course, unless there's some dire emergency at the clinic.'

'Brill.' Rupert turned to Daisy. 'You won't be gone long, Mum, will you? Now that Adam's going there won't be anyone to talk to. And I'll let you have a go at my game,' he added generously, unconscious of any irony.

'Mega,' said Daisy, managing a small laugh. 'I look forward to that.'

'Now,' said Adam when, a few minutes later, he and Daisy were outside the hospital and making for the car park. 'Tell me all, love.' He took her hand. 'What's worrying you? Why the sudden anxiety?'

'Us, Adam, you and me.' She took a deep breath and said firmly, 'Look, I don't think I should marry you; it isn't fair, even if Rupert approves.'

He stopped abruptly and stared at her. 'Good God, woman, whyever not?'

She stared back at him, unexpected tears glistening in her eyes. 'Because,' she whispered, 'you'd get such a bad deal. It wouldn't be fair, and one day you'd regret it.'

He turned to face her and put his hands on her

shoulders. 'What the hell do you mean by that?' he asked, astonishment written all over his face.

'Well, you'd be giving so much to us—care, security, a home—but what have we got to give in return? Nothing.'

'Nothing! My dear Daisy, don't talk rubbish.' He dropped his hands from her shoulders. 'Look, we can't talk here; let's get to the car.'

He took her elbow and steered her to the new Range Rover that had replaced the one involved in the accident. An understated forest-green, it looked elegant and tough at the same time. Just like Adam, thought Daisy abstractedly as he settled her in the passenger seat.

'Now,' he said briskly when he was seated beside her. 'To repeat myself—don't talk rubbish. What am I getting in return for you marrying me? The short answer to that is your love, Daisy, something that I've waited for for years. Everything else is a bonus.'

'A bonus?'

'Yes, having a ready-made family—a delightful, cheerful, intelligent stepson to whom I already feel incredibly close, and a clever, informed, loving wife who understands the pressures that a doctor is under. A perfect companion. What more could I ask for?'

'Someone not quite so dependent. I've no savings to speak of, no house to sell, a few pieces of quite nice furniture, a small legacy from my aunt, that's all,' said Daisy, clasping her hands tightly in her lap until the knuckles showed white. 'And Rupert *is* a bright, happy little boy, but he's going to need a lot of care over the next few months, and if his foot and leg don't mend properly he's going to need more operations over the years. He might be permanently disabled, Adam.'

'And he might not. But if he is, I want to be around to look after him and you. As for the rest, you're talking about material things, Daisy, and they're irrelevant. I don't need them. I'm lucky—I've more than enough of this world's good for the three of us, or even any other offspring we might have.' He gave her a quirky smile and said drily, 'I always expected to support my wife, you know, and if the worst comes to the worst I can always send you out to work.'

Daisy gave a shaky laugh and, jutting out her neat, determined chin, said in a small but firm voice, 'I might *want* to go out to work and continue with my career; had you thought of that?'

'Indeed I have. And I see no reason why you shouldn't, if that's what you want. We can always arrange care for Rupert or an extended family. As long as you take time off occasionally to share yourself with me, I see no reason why you shouldn't have a career.' He turned and cupped her face in both hands. 'Is that one of your fears, Daisy—that you would lose your independence if you married me?' His dark eyes bored into hers.

She looked back at him steadily. 'Perhaps,' she murmured. 'You see, although I had Aunt Mary, I have been managing on my own for so long and I value my independence. But it isn't only that. Oh, Adam, I'm so afraid that, whatever you feel now, the time might come when you think of Rupert and me as a burden. I couldn't bear that. You might even start blaming me again for my broken marriage to Matthew. You seemed to hate me so much at one time.'

'Oh, my dear love, don't say that. I never hated you, not in my heart. I never stopped loving you. But I had to come to terms with the fact that if I believed you I had to accept that Matthew had been lying to me and, what was more, that he was capable of behaving so abominably towards you; that was the hardest thing to swallow. That he was weak, a gambler, a drunk even, I could understand—just—but cruelty? Never. I resisted the idea. And yet I knew that you were telling me the truth. I never really doubted you. It was quite clear that you were, and are, a woman of great integrity. I was fighting myself, not you. There'll never be any recriminations, I promise you.'

'Oh, Adam, my dearest Adam, are you sure? Do you mean that?'

'With all my heart.' He leaned towards her and kissed her long and tenderly on her wide, generous mouth. Then he said softly, 'Daisy, I want you as my wife and Rupert as my son to love and care for always. Go and tell him about us now; don't waste any more time. Let's put love—ours for each other and his for me—on the line. I have the utmost faith in his intuition. The three of us belong together. Now, go and talk to Rupert, and phone later if there's any news to give me.'

They kissed again, a long, deep, satisfying kiss, full of restrained passion, then he helped her from the car and they said their goodbyes. A few minutes later, she watched him drive away until he was out of sight.

CHAPTER TWELVE

'Go AND talk to Rupert,' Adam had said, but it was easier said than done to find an opportunity to have a serious conversation with him.

When Daisy arrived back in the ward it was to find that his bed had been pushed into the playroom, where he was watching television with some of the other youngsters. And soon after children's television had finished it was suppertime, and then time to tuck Rupert up for the night and return to her own room.

After the switchback emotions of the day, she had a restless night, waking at intervals to wonder what response Rupert would make when he heard about her and Adam. In the small hours of the morning her hopes that he would welcome Adam as his stepfather dwindled. In spite of the rapport that existed between them, surely it was much too soon for him to take the idea aboard? It was too much to ask of him.

Unhappily she stared into the darkness, visualising a bleak future without Adam's constant, loving presence, unable even to take comfort in the thought that Rupert might eventually come round to the idea. Her confidence, fired yesterday by Adam's certainty that all would be well, drained away and she felt helpless and lonely.

She got up early and showered, dressed and had her breakfast in an almost belligerent mood, hell-bent on talking to Rupert. She wasn't sure how she would broach the subject, but she was determined to discuss the future with him before the morning was out.

He had just been bed-bathed and made comfortable when she arrived in the ward. It was warm, and he was sitting on top of the bedclothes, his plaster-splinted legs, with their little observation windows, splayed out in front of him.

He gave her a wide but, she thought, rather tentative smile as she approached, his dark brown eyes, so like Adam's, serious, and his blond hair, so like her own, neatly brushed and gleaming, a golden cap. He looked the picture of health, not like a child just recoving from injury and trauma.

Daisy's heart turned over. With a flush of maternal pride she had to admit to herself that as a product of a one-parent family, and not discounting Aunt Mary's help, he had turned out rather well. A happy, contented, well-rounded child. Don't let me spoil things and upset him, she prayed silently.

'Hi, Mum,' he said as she kissed him good morning and he returned her kiss. 'I want to talk to you about something. Sort of in private.' He sounded, for a moment, very adult. 'Can you pull the curtains, 'cos I don't want Gary and the others to come over?'

Staring at him in surprise, she automatically did as he requested, pulling the curtains round the bed. What on earth did he want to say to her that required privacy? How strange that he wanted to talk to her as urgently as she wanted to talk to him. Obviously her business would have to keep. Was he frightened about something? Had the doctors been to see him and given him bad news? No, it couldn't be anything like that; she would have been informed, and anyway, he looked solemn but not distressed.

She pulled up a chair and sat down, resting her arms on the bed, her eyes on a level with his. 'Well, I'm ready and waiting and all ears,' she said evenly. 'I'm dying to know what this is all about.'

Rupert laid a hand on her arm for a moment. 'Mum,' he began in a low, serious voice, 'can I ask you something?'

'Anything, son; you know you've always been able to ask me anything.' She smiled at him encouragingly.

He frowned and then said slowly, picking his words carefully, 'Well, it's about Adam.'

'Adam?' she repeated blankly. She stared at Rupert and he stared back. Everything seemed to go quiet; the ward sounds from beyond the curtains receded. Why did he sound so solemn? What on earth could he have to say about Adam? Why was he so deadly serious, cautious, as if he was about to say something that would displease her? Had he suddenly sensed the love between her and Adam and resented it? Was he testing her reaction? She couldn't begin to guess. There was only one way to find out. 'Go on,' she said quietly, raising another smile to reassure him. 'Ask away.'

'Do you like Adam, Mum—a lot, I mean?'

She had no idea what he wanted to hear, but it was a straightforward question deserving a straightforward answer.

She took a deep breath. 'Yes, I do,' she said.

'As much as you liked my dad?'

'Oh, yes, quite as much,' she said firmly.

He hesitated, and then asked awkwardly, 'And do you, well, sort of love him?'

Daisy's heart beat a tattoo. How ironic—her son questioning her about her love life. How much had he guessed about her feelings for Adam? What was he hoping to hear? 'Love him?' Her voice trembled. 'Hey, what is this—the third degree?'

Rupert looked hurt. 'Don't joke, Mum; it's not funny,' he said stiffly. 'I want to know. It's important.'

Feeling guilty, Daisy said, 'Sorry; I wasn't really joking, Rupert. You just surprised me. You sound so grown-up. And for what it's worth, yes, I do love him very much.'

'And does he love you?'

'I happen to know that he does. In fact he loves us both.' She took another deep breath. Well, here goes, she thought; now you've got to come clean; no more prevaricating. 'Adam wants to marry me, darling. He wants to take care of us both, now and always.'

For a few seconds they stared at each other in silence. Daisy held her breath. She felt slightly sick. Her stomach churned. What was Rupert's reaction going to be? Would he be for or against her marrying Adam?

And then, as she watched his impassive face, slowly, very slowly, she saw his lips curve into a wide smile and his sombre brown eyes light up. 'Oh, Mum,' he said in a voice that trembled slightly, 'that's brill, mega.' He leaned forward, kissed her hard on the cheek and then sat back, looking flushed and embarrassed. 'It'll be great,' he added gruffly, 'to have a father of my own. Do you think he'd mind if I called him Dad?'

'Oh, Rupert, love, he'd be thrilled to bits if you did that.'

Adam arrived early that afternoon, as he had on the previous day, only this time Daisy was not on the bed but sitting in the armchair waiting for him.

As he tapped and entered, she turned a studiously straight face to greet him. He stood just inside the door, casually elegant in fawn cords, tweedy jacket and lemon-coloured cashmere sweater. He closed the door and smiled at her.

'Ah,' he said softly. 'You've got news for me! I can see it in your face. You've told Rupert about us, and. . .?'

'And. . . Oh, Adam!' She couldn't hide her happiness any longer; her eyes blazed with joy. 'He's over the moon about it.' She giggled like a schoolgirl. 'In fact, I not only have my son's permission to marry you, Dr Torrence, but have almost been ordered to do so.'

His smile turned into a broad grin. 'I told you,' he said, his deep voice sounding smug, gravelly, 'that there was something very special between us. We understand each other. Oh, Daisy!' In a few easy strides he crossed the room, scooped her up into his arms and sat down with her on his lap. 'I love you, Daisy Marchment,' he murmured, gently rubbing his nose against hers and nuzzling her neck.

'And I love you,' she breathed. 'So very much.' She ran her fingers through the thick mass of black hair from the peak on his high forehead to the nape of his neck. 'Kiss me, please,' she whispered. 'I can't believe what's happened. I can't believe that you want to mary me and that Rupert wants me to marry you. It all seems a bit unreal. I feel as if I'm floating on air.'

Adam kissed her firmly on the mouth, cupped her face in his hands, and said gently, 'Then let me bring you back to earth and formally ask you to marry me. I hope you will accept this, my darling, even though it is second-hand.' He produced a small box from the top pocket of his jacket.

'I've been carrying this around for a long time. It belonged to my paternal grandmother. It was her engagement ring, especially designed for her by my grandfather, who adored her. Like you, she had violet-blue eyes and daffodil-blonde hair when she was young. And like you, dear heart, she was widowed when young and brought up a family on her own. True, she hadn't money problems, but in every other way she was your kindred spirit—courageous, generous and a wonderful mother.'

He snapped open the box to reveal a sparkling oblong dark blue sapphire, framed by a double row of tiny, glittering blue-white diamonds in an antique claw setting, on a wide band of platinum.

Daisy stared at it. 'Oh, Adam, it's utterly beautiful! Are you sure that your grandmother would want me to have it? It must be very valuable, a family heirloom.'

'She left it to me to give to the woman I wanted to make my wife, and that woman is you, Daisy—has always been you.' He brushed a feather-light kiss across her cheek and his dark, luminous brown eyes, so close to hers, were alight with love and tenderness.

He took the glowing sapphire from the box and lifted up her left hand, and as he did so Matthew's wedding-ring glimmered on her third finger. 'Oh, I'd forgotten that,' she said, flushing slightly. 'I've always worn it for Rupert's sake.'

Adam said firmly, 'And quite right, too.' He smiled into her eyes. 'May I suggest that from now on you wear it on your right hand?'

'Yes, please, if you don't mind.'

'Of course I don't mind, my darling.'

She watched, with a little catch at her heart-strings, as slowly, smoothly, with infinite gentleness, he slid the ring off her left hand and on to her right. He brushed her bare ring finger with his lips. 'There.' He slipped the precious sapphire on to her slender finger. 'At last, my beautiful Daisy, we are officially engaged to be married.'

He gave her a quirky grin and raised his eyebrows. 'And, at the risk of sounding pompous,' he added, 'it'll be my privilege to love and cherish you and Rupert for the rest of my days.'

'Till death us do part,' she murmured.

'As you say.' He kissed her gently, then cupped his hands about her chin and feasted his eyes upon her face. 'Happy, love?' he asked huskily.

'Truly happy,' she said. 'Or, as Rupert would say, *mega*!'

Christmas Journeys

4 new short romances all wrapped up in 1 sparkling volume.

Join four delightful couples as they journey home for the festive season—and discover the true meaning of Christmas...that love is the best gift of all!

A Man To Live For - Emma Richmond

Yule Tide - Catherine George

Mistletoe Kisses - Lynsey Stevens

Christmas Charade - Kay Gregory

Available: November 1995 **Price: £4.99**

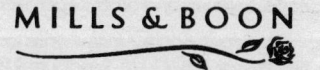

MILLS & BOON

Available from WH Smith, John Menzies, Volume One, Forbuoys, Martins, Tesco, Asda, Safeway and other paperback stockists.

MILLS & BOON

LOVE ON CALL

The books for enjoyment this month are:

A FAMILIAR STRANGER	Caroline Anderson
ENCHANTING SURGEON	Marion Lennox
DOWNLAND CLINIC	Margaret O'Neill
A MATTER OF ETHICS	Patricia Robertson

Treats in store!

Watch next month for the following absorbing stories:

DR WENTWORTH'S BABIES	Frances Crowne
CRISIS IN CALLASAY	Drusilla Douglas
A PROMISE TO PROTECT	Abigail Gordon
A TEMPORARY LOVER	Carol Wood

Available from W.H. Smith, John Menzies, Forbuoys, Martins, Tesco, Asda, Safeway and other paperback stockists.

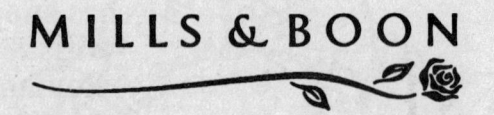

Readers in South Africa - write to:
IBS, Private Bag X3010, Randburg 2125.

WIN A years supply of Mills & Boon Romances — absolutely free!

Would you like to win a years supply of heartwarming and passionate romances? Well, you can and they're FREE! All you have to do is complete the wordsearch puzzle below and send it to us by 30th April 1996. The first 5 correct entries picked after that date will win a years supply of Mills & Boon Romance novels (six books every month – worth over £100). What could be easier?

STOCKHOLM	PARIS	HELSINKI	ANKARA
REYKJAVIK	LONDON	ROME	AMSTERDAM
COPENHAGEN	PRAGUE	VIENNA	OSLO
MADRID	ATHENS	LIMA	

N	O	L	S	O	P	A	R	I	S
E	Q	U	V	A	F	R	O	K	T
G	C	L	I	M	A	A	M	N	O
A	T	H	E	N	S	K	E	I	C
H	L	O	N	D	O	N	H	S	K
N	S	H	N	R	I	A	O	L	H
E	D	M	A	D	R	I	D	E	O
P	R	A	G	U	E	U	Y	H	L
O	A	M	S	T	E	R	D	A	M
C	R	E	Y	K	J	A	V	I	K

Please turn over for details on how to enter ➤

How to enter

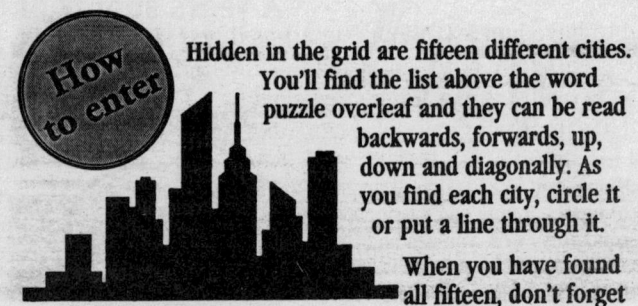

Hidden in the grid are fifteen different cities. You'll find the list above the word puzzle overleaf and they can be read backwards, forwards, up, down and diagonally. As you find each city, circle it or put a line through it.

When you have found all fifteen, don't forget to fill in your name and address in the space provided below and pop this page in an envelope (you don't need a stamp) and post it today. Hurry – competition ends 30th April 1996.

Mills & Boon Capital Wordsearch
FREEPOST
Croydon
Surrey
CR9 3WZ

Are you a Reader Service Subscriber?   Yes ☐   No ☐

Ms/Mrs/Miss/Mr _____

Address _____

_____

_____ Postcode _____

One application per household.

You may be mailed with other offers from other reputable companies as a result of this application. If you would prefer not to receive such offers, please tick box. ☐

COMP495
D